Paradise in Penang

In a rapt voice that was like the song of a bird, Anona said: "How can you . . . love me . . . when you . . . do not even . . . know who . . . I am?"

Lord Selwyn smiled.

"The only thing that matters is that I have found you, when I was certain you did not exist."

She looked at him, and he thought it was impossible for anyone to look so radiant.

"When will you marry me, my darling? I want you with me—and alone!"

For a moment Anona just looked at him.

Then, like a shadow moving over the moon, the radiance faded from her face.

"No!" she said. "No, no! You . . . must not . . . say that!"

A Camfield Novel of Love
by Barbara Cartland

"*Barbara Cartland's novels are all distinguished by their intelligence, good sense, and good nature . . .*"
— ROMANTIC TIMES

"*Who could give better advice on how to keep your romance going strong than the world's most famous romance novelist, Barbara Cartland?*"

Camfield Place,
Hatfield
Hertfordshire,
England

Dearest Reader,

Camfield Novels of Love mark a very exciting era of my books with Jove. They have already published nearly two hundred of my titles since they became my first publisher in America, and now all my original paperback romances in the future will be published exclusively by them.

As you already know, Camfield Place in Hertfordshire is my home, which originally existed in 1275, but was rebuilt in 1867 by the grandfather of Beatrix Potter.

It was here in this lovely house, with the best view in the county, that she wrote *The Tale of Peter Rabbit*. Mr. McGregor's garden is exactly as she described it. The door in the wall that the fat little rabbit could not squeeze underneath and the goldfish pool where the white cat sat twitching its tail are still there.

I had Camfield Place blessed when I came here in 1950 and was so happy with my husband until he died, and now with my children and grandchildren, that I know the atmosphere is filled with love and we have all been very lucky.

It is easy here to write of love and I know you will enjoy the Camfield Novels of Love. Their plots are definitely exciting and the covers very romantic. They come to you, like all my books, with love.

Bless you,

CAMFIELD NOVELS OF LOVE

by Barbara Cartland

THE POOR GOVERNESS
WINGED VICTORY
LUCKY IN LOVE
LOVE AND THE MARQUIS
A MIRACLE IN MUSIC
LIGHT OF THE GODS
BRIDE TO A BRIGAND
LOVE COMES WEST
A WITCH'S SPELL
SECRETS
THE STORMS OF LOVE
MOONLIGHT ON THE
  SPHINX
WHITE LILAC
REVENGE OF THE HEART
THE ISLAND OF LOVE
THERESA AND A TIGER
LOVE IS HEAVEN
MIRACLE FOR A MADONNA
A VERY UNUSUAL WIFE
THE PERIL AND THE
  PRINCE
ALONE AND AFRAID
TEMPTATIONS OF A
  TEACHER
ROYAL PUNISHMENT
THE DEVILISH DECEPTION
PARADISE FOUND
LOVE IS A GAMBLE
A VICTORY FOR LOVE

LOOK WITH LOVE
NEVER FORGET LOVE
HELGA IN HIDING
SAFE AT LAST
HAUNTED
CROWNED WITH LOVE
ESCAPE
THE DEVIL DEFEATED
THE SECRET OF THE
  MOSQUE
A DREAM IN SPAIN
THE LOVE TRAP
LISTEN TO LOVE
THE GOLDEN CAGE
LOVE CASTS OUT FEAR
A WORLD OF LOVE
DANCING ON A RAINBOW
LOVE JOINS THE CLANS
AN ANGEL RUNS AWAY
FORCED TO MARRY
BEWILDERED IN BERLIN
WANTED—A WEDDING
  RING
THE EARL ESCAPES
STARLIGHT OVER TUNIS
THE LOVE PUZZLE
LOVE AND KISSES
SAPPHIRES IN SIAM
A CARETAKER OF LOVE
SECRETS OF THE HEART

RIDING IN THE SKY
LOVERS IN LISBON
LOVE IS INVINCIBLE
THE GODDESS OF LOVE
AN ADVENTURE OF LOVE
THE HERB FOR HAPPINESS
ONLY A DREAM
SAVED BY LOVE
LITTLE TONGUES OF FIRE
A CHIEFTAIN FINDS LOVE
THE LOVELY LIAR
THE PERFUME OF THE
  GODS
A KNIGHT IN PARIS
REVENGE IS SWEET
THE PASSIONATE PRINCESS
SOLITA AND THE SPIES
THE PERFECT PEARL
LOVE IS A MAZE
A CIRCUS FOR LOVE
THE TEMPLE OF LOVE
THE BARGAIN BRIDE
THE HAUNTED HEART
REAL LOVE OR FAKE
KISS FROM A STRANGER
A VERY SPECIAL LOVE
THE NECKLACE OF LOVE
A REVOLUTION OF LOVE
THE MARQUIS WINS
LOVE IS THE KEY

Other Books by Barbara Cartland

THE ADVENTURER
AGAIN THIS RAPTURE
BARBARA CARTLAND'S
  BOOK OF BEAUTY AND
  HEALTH
BLUE HEATHER
BROKEN BARRIERS
THE CAPTIVE HEART
THE COIN OF LOVE
THE COMPLACENT WIFE
COUNT THE STARS
DESIRE OF THE HEART
DESPERATE DEFIANCE
THE DREAM WITHIN
ELIZABETHAN LOVER
THE ENCHANTED WALTZ
THE ENCHANTING EVIL
ESCAPE FROM PASSION
FOR ALL ETERNITY
A GOLDEN GONDOLA
A HAZARD OF HEARTS
A HEART IS BROKEN

THE IRRESISTIBLE BUCK
THE KISS OF PARIS
THE KISS OF THE DEVIL
A KISS OF SILK
THE KNAVE OF HEARTS
THE LEAPING FLAME
LIGHTS OF LOVE
THE LITTLE PRETENDER
LOST ENCHANTMENT
LOVE AT FORTY
LOVE FORBIDDEN
LOVE IN HIDING
LOVE IS THE ENEMY
LOVE ME FOREVER
LOVE TO THE RESCUE
LOVE UNDER FIRE
THE MAGIC OF HONEY
METTERNICH THE
  PASSIONATE DIPLOMAT
MONEY, MAGIC AND
  MARRIAGE
THE RELUCTANT BRIDE

THE SCANDALOUS LIFE OF
  KING CAROL
THE SECRET FEAR
THE SMUGGLED HEART
A SONG OF LOVE
STARS IN MY HEART
STOLEN HALO
SWEET ENCHANTRESS
SWEET PUNISHMENT
THEFT OF A HEART
THE THIEF OF LOVE
THIS TIME IT'S LOVE
TOUCH A STAR
TOWARDS THE STARS
THE UNKNOWN HEART
WE DANCED ALL
  NIGHT
THE WINGS OF ECSTASY
THE WINGS OF LOVE
WINGS ON MY HEART
WOMAN, THE ENIGMA

A NEW CAMFIELD NOVEL OF LOVE BY

BARBARA CARTLAND

Paradise in Penang

JOVE BOOKS, NEW YORK

PARADISE IN PENANG

A Jove Book/published by arrangement with
the author
PRINTING HISTORY
Jove edition/November 1990

ISBN: 0-515-10448-5

Jove Books are published by The Berkley Publishing Group,
200 Madison Avenue, New York, New York 10016.
The name ''Jove'' and the ''J'' logo
are trademarks belonging to Jove Publications, Inc.

PRINTED IN THE UNITED STATES OF AMERICA

10 9 8 7 6 5 4 3 2 1

Author's Note

PENANG is a tiny, turtle-shaped island at the Northern extremity of the Straits of Malacca and is one of the most beautiful places in the world.

Washed by the warm, clear waters of the Indian Ocean, it is fringed by golden beaches and coconut palms.

It was to Penang that brave and adventurous men came, after it was discovered by the English Captain Francis Light in 1786.

They made huge fortunes, built enormous mansions in the English Style, and settled in happily with the Malayans and the Chinese.

At the time I have written of in this book two infamous Secret Societies were being hunted by the Authorities.

They committed murder, and fought dangerous duels for the new-found wealth.

Captain Light was offered the Pulau Pinang by the Sultan Abdullah of Kedah in exchange for active intervention against his Siamese enemies.

Penang was of great importance to the East India Company and became an important trading post for the whole Empire.

It is now a holiday resort, but there are many monuments, houses, and buildings to remind one of its fascinating history and I hope a fascinating future.

chapter one

1869

THE train came into Victoria Station and Lord Selwyn stepped out with a sigh of relief.

He was home!

There was no carriage waiting to meet him, but fortunately travelling with him was a French Diplomat.

He was to be met by a carriage sent by his Embassy.

"May I give you a lift, My Lord?" he asked.

"I would be most grateful," Lord Selwyn replied. "As I have already told you, I left sooner than I expected and did not have time to notify my Secretary that I was returning earlier than I had arranged."

The Diplomat smiled.

"I have always been told, My Lord, that that is a dangerous thing to do."

Lord Selwyn laughed.

"Not as far as I am concerned, but of course you are right in principle."

They stepped into the Embassy carriage.

Lord Selwyn noted it was not only very smart, but also was drawn by two well-bred horses.

They were not the equal of his own. At the same time, they were a credit to whoever had purchased them.

As he sank down against the well-padded back-seat, he thought that tonight he would see Maisie Brambury.

She had been in his mind ever since he left England.

Then while he was in Paris he had made what he knew was the most important decision of his life.

He would get married!

For years he had fought against what at first had been hints from his family, then pleadings, for him to be married.

He could not imagine why there should be any hurry for him to do so.

Except, of course, that he was distinguished, extremely wealthy, and owned one of the finest Georgian houses in the country.

It was obvious, therefore, that sooner or later he must have an heir.

He had decided that the idea of being tied down was abhorrent to him.

He wanted to be free, untrammelled, and definitely unencumbered by a wife.

He had gone to Paris on a very delicate diplomatic mission assigned to him by Lord Clarendon, Secretary of State for Foreign Affairs.

He had been determined to forget Lady Brambury.

Paris, he knew, would be full of women who wanted to flatter him into spending his money.

At the same time, they made sure that he felt every penny of it had been well spent.

Although he had adhered strictly to the business in hand, which was characteristic of him, his evenings were free.

It was then he searched for the attractive Courtesans whom he had met on his last visit.

They welcomed him with open arms, and he went from party to party and inevitably from bed to bed.

It was only yesterday morning that he had decided that enough was enough.

If he was honest, and he usually was honest with himself, he had to admit that the magic of Paris had this time not been there.

He had forced himself to enjoy what in the past had been spontaneous excitement, what the French called very rightly *joie de vivre*.

At first he had asked what was wrong.

He finally had to admit that instead of the alluring dark eyes looking passionately into his, he could see only the blue of Lady Brambury's.

He could hear only her voice, soft and childlike, as she talked to him.

"I am being a fool!" he told himself, and drank a little more champagne.

Nothing the French could provide seemed now to satisfy him.

The food he had enjoyed at the parties was superlative and even better when he took some Charmer to Maxim's or Le Grand Vefour.

No one, he thought, could be more alluring than the French *Demi-Mondaines*.

They were *chic*, and they were witty with a fascination that was all their own.

They made every man feel like a King.

But all he could hear was a little voice saying:

"I am so . . . alone and the . . . Social World . . . frightens me!"

Two blue eyes looked at him helplessly.

He felt he wanted to protect Maisie, and there was only one way by which he could do so.

"But marriage is not for me!"

He wondered how often he had said those words to his relatives, to his men-friends, and to too many women for him to count.

He had everything that he could possibly want.

He was never lonely in his impressive house in the country, or in the one in Park Lane.

As he was exceedingly intelligent, he enjoyed reading.

While his contemporaries rushed to their Clubs rather than be alone at home, Lord Selwyn could sit reading in his Library long into the night.

"You must be careful, dearest, not to ruin your eyes," his mother had said when she was alive. "You will not look so handsome if you have to wear spectacles!"

Lord Selwyn had laughed.

There were many years for him to enjoy reading, he thought, before his eyes began to fail.

Reading books gave him as much pleasure as did a beautiful woman.

Moreover, he often thought cynically, they lasted longer.

All his love-affairs came to an end simply because he found there was nothing to talk about except love.

The English language was regrettably limited on the subject.

The women who gave him their favours were undeniably beautiful, and had figures like young goddesses.

But while his body responded to their beauty, he found his brain being critical, also, although it was a strange word, "deprived."

When he thought of marriage, he realised it would be impossible for him to listen to banal conversation.

It was what he would have to do from first thing in the morning to last thing at night.

Even his most witty and amusing mistresses had a way of expecting him to laugh at the same joke they had told him before or to pay them the same compliments over and over again.

"What am I looking for? What do I want?" he asked.

There was no answer.

When he looked at Maisie Brambury he thought she was different.

To begin with, she looked very young.

He had just finished an *affaire de coeur* with a woman a little older than himself.

Maisie was therefore a delightful contrast.

She was, he thought, like the small cherubs he had seen carved and painted in Bavarian Churches.

At first he could hardly believe that she was aged twenty-four, to which she admitted.

Then, when he learnt her history, he understood.

Maisie had been married when she was eighteen to Lord Brambury, who was one of the most important figures at Court.

That he was sixty when he first saw Maisie was considered unimportant beside the fact that he was so distinguished.

He held many posts including that of Lord Lieutenant of Huntingdonshire, and was extremely wealthy.

He had been married before.

His first wife had died, having unfortunately failed to provide him with any children.

When he proposed marriage to the daughter of a well-born country Squire, he was being sensible in making sure that time that he had an heir.

Maisie's parents were completely overcome that their daughter should have received such an offer.

Because she was very pretty, they had hoped she might marry well.

They had planned to take her to London for the Season.

But before they could do so, she met Lord Brambury.

Like many an older man had done before him, he fell head-over-heels in love with a very much younger woman.

Casting discretion to the winds, he refused to listen to an inner voice which told him he was too old for her.

Maisie was everything of which he had dreamed.

She was young, healthy, and of good country stock, and would give him the son he wanted.

Maisie had little say in what was happening.

She was told she was the luckiest girl in the world, that every one of her contemporaries would envy her.

She was swept up the aisle of St. George's Hanover Square.

She had always imagined she would be married in the little Church which stood on her father's estate.

But Lord Brambury was too important.

"You will understand, my dear," he said, "that Her Majesty the Queen will be present at the Church, and a large number of Statesmen, Courtiers, and Diplomats will attend the Ceremony."

He clinched the matter quite easily.

He announced that the Reception would take place in the large house in Grosvenor Square which he had occupied for nearly thirty years.

Maisie was never asked if she agreed or disagreed with all that was planned.

She was told only what had been arranged.

This meant that Lord Brambury had given his orders and all her father and mother had to do was to accept them.

Because it was undoubtedly the most important wedding of the Season, everybody wished to be present.

St. George's Church was full to overflowing.

The huge Reception rooms of the house in Grosvenor Square were packed.

When his friends saw Maisie they could understand why Lord Brambury was so infatuated with anyone so lovely.

She looked like a piece of Dresden china.

It is true that one or two of them sniggered that "there is no fool like an old fool!"

But they kept their voices low, having no wish to offend a man who had the Queen's ear.

Lord Brambury had in the whole of his successful life never put a foot wrong.

To Maisie everything seemed unreal.

It was as if she had stepped from the School-Room into a maelstrom.

Lord Brambury had wished to get married as quickly as possible.

Maisie was therefore hurried from one Dressmaker to another.

She found it extremely tiring to stand for hours being fitted for gown after gown.

There were parties almost every night.

The Brambury family was very large, and they all wished to ingratiate themselves with the head of it.

Invitations to luncheons, dinners, Receptions, and Assemblies poured in.

Maisie's father and mother enjoyed every moment of it.

But Maisie herself saw very little of her future husband.

"You will understand, my dear," he said, "that before I take you away on our honeymoon I have a thousand-and-one things to attend to."

He smiled before he added:

"I have always found that if I want something well done, I have to do it myself."

Maisie had, of course, agreed, and in a way she was relieved.

She was, in fact, rather frightened of this large and imposing man whose hair was turning grey.

She wondered vaguely what he would expect of her when she was his wife.

She had no one she could ask.

Her mother had always treated her as if she were a very young child.

Her father made no secret of the fact that he was disappointed she was not a boy.

She had been educated by a series of Governesses who never stayed long.

They had found it boring living in the depths of the country.

8

They had no chance of going to London or to any other large town.

"I am sorry," they would say at the end of a year, "but I do feel as if I am buried here."

Maisie's parents could not understand.

"After all, the woman has a very nice bedroom!" Maisie's mother said indignantly. "And the School-Room gets all the sunshine."

Governesses came and went.

Each one started the History lessons with Hengist and Horsa so that Maisie never got beyond Richard Coeur de Lyons.

She found History boring and Geography worse.

She learnt, however, not to make any protests but to look as if she were listening wide-eyed to what they were saying to her.

Nine times out of ten she got away with it.

It was the same expression she put on when Lord Brambury talked to her before they were married.

It was the same expression she assumed when they set off amid a shower of rose-petals and rice to the Station.

They were to travel in Lord Brambury's private coach to Huntingdonshire.

He had planned to spend the first week of their honeymoon at his ancestral home.

Then they would go to his Hunting-Lodge in Leicestershire which he had not used for a long time.

He had, in fact, given up hunting ten years ago.

The house was partly Jacobean and stood on five-hundred acres of good Leicestershire soil.

Maisie learnt that it had been in his family for three generations.

"I would never part with it," he told Maisie's father. "It is comfortable and quiet, and I know we shall not be disturbed on our honeymoon."

It was during the train journey that Maisie thought her husband looked rather flushed.

She had been enjoying the train because she had never been in a private carriage before.

"Are you not feeling well?" she asked in a concerned voice, which pleased him.

"I am quite all right," he replied. "It was very hot in the Church, and even hotter at the Reception."

She poured him out a glass of champagne and he drank it thirstily.

"You were a credit to me," he said with satisfaction, "and you looked exactly as I wanted you to—beautiful!"

"I hoped you would like my gown," Maisie replied. "It was very expensive!"

"You need not worry about that in the future," Lord Brambury answered in a thick voice.

He drank some more champagne which seemed to make his voice even thicker.

Maisie had described to Lord Selwyn what had happened when they arrived at Brambury Hall.

"We had . . . dinner," she said, "and I thought Arthur . . . looked a little . . . strange. He ate very . . . little but . . . drank rather a lot."

Her voice trembled and was almost inaudible.

Lord Selwyn was listening.

At the same time, he was thinking how lovely Maisie's pink-and-white skin was.

He noticed that her eye-lashes curled up like a child's, dark at the roots, fading into gold.

"After . . . dinner we . . . went up to . . . bed," Maisie went on in a hesitating voice.

She stopped speaking and clasped her hands together. Lord Selwyn said gently:

"I do not want you to upset yourself."

"But . . . I wish . . . you to . . . know," Maisie said. "I . . . have never . . . told this before . . . to anybody."

She looked away from him and he thought because she was shy it was very alluring.

"I . . . I got into . . . bed," she said in a voice he could hardly hear, "then . . . Arthur came into . . . my room."

She drew in her breath as if she could see it all happening again.

"He . . . he walked . . . towards me . . . then . . . just before he . . . reached the bed . . . he made a strange . . . sound in his . . . throat."

She gave a little sob.

"As I put out my . . . hands . . . towards him he . . . collapsed and . . . fell forward."

There was silence until Lord Selwyn said:

"He had suffered a stroke."

Maisie nodded.

"It was . . . terrible! I cannot tell you . . . how terrible it was! And the Doctors could do . . . nothing to . . . help him."

The tragedy was, Lord Selwyn thought, that Lord Brambury did not die at once.

He remained a helpless cripple for five years—five years when there was nothing Maisie could do but be near him and listen to the Doctors as they came and went.

The Doctors tried to give her hope.

11

But they spoke in a way which made her know her husband's recovery was unlikely.

"It is difficult to put into words how sorry I am for you," Lord Selwyn said.

"I knew . . . you would . . . understand," Maisie replied simply.

As she spoke he wanted to make up to her for all the years she had wasted her beauty.

She had seen no one but Doctors and Nurses.

The Brambury relatives visited the house occasionally, feeling it their duty to enquire after the head of the family.

Then, when Lord Brambury finally died, Maisie was free.

At the same time, because the years had passed her by, she had no idea what to do with herself.

"My father suggested I should come to London," she said. "At first I was rather . . . frightened because I knew . . . nobody and was . . . afraid of being alone."

She went on to tell him that it was Lord Brambury's sister, herself a widow, who chaperoned her.

Lady Elton, who was five years older than her brother, moved into Grosvenor Square.

The house had been shut up for five years, but it was soon a hive of activity.

The Brambury relations were only too willing to let a rich young widow entertain them and anybody else they wanted to introduce as a suitable friend.

There was no need for Maisie to exert herself in any way.

Her relatives were quite prepared to engage servants for her.

Lord Brambury's Secretary had run his Master's

houses and properties extremely well while he lay unconscious.

"What makes me afraid," Maisie confided to Lord Selwyn, "is that I may make a second mistake."

She paused a moment before continuing:

"I know now that it was . . . wrong of me to marry anyone so very much . . . older than . . . myself, but if I had said 'No,' nobody would have . . . listened to . . . me!"

Lord Selwyn understood.

He was also astute enough to realise that Maisie was wooing him and wanted him as her second husband.

It did not occur to him that there was any advantage.

Lord Brambury had left her a fortune as well as the Dower House in Huntingdonshire and the house in Grosvenor Square.

The Ancestral home had gone to the new holder of the title, a nephew.

He made it quite clear that he was not interested in his uncle's widow.

He required her only to vacate the house as quickly as possible.

As it happened, she was only too eager to leave what had seemed to her a Morgue ever since her wedding-day.

She had been in London for six months before she met Lord Selwyn.

He had heard about her but had not been particularly interested.

He was told she was very lovely, but so were a great number of other women, especially the one in whom he was interested at the moment.

When they did meet, however, he found himself amused and intrigued by the story of her marriage.

A great number of people were talking about it.

He was also told that she was hailed as an important hostess.

When he first saw her, he was inclined to laugh at the idea.

She was so small, so childlike, standing at the top of the stairs receiving her guests.

He thought for a moment it must be a joke.

Then, when she looked at him with her baby blue eyes, he found himself at first interested, then captivated.

'She is certainly original!' he thought.

Several people had a great deal to say because the marriage had never been consummated.

"A widow *and* a virgin!" they laughed. "That, if nothing else, is certainly unusual!"

Lord Selwyn received invitation after invitation to the house in Grosvenor Square.

He realised he was on Lady Brambury's guest-list.

Only when she asked him to dine with just two other guests present had he been sure what she intended.

The other two guests were elderly and left early.

Maisie and Lord Selwyn had sat talking in the very glamorous and comfortable Sitting-Room until midnight.

If that had happened with any other woman, Lord Selwyn would have known exactly where he stood and what was expected of him.

But with Maisie he felt unsure of himself.

He felt that if he suggested he should become her lover, she would be extremely shocked.

She might refuse to see him, and that was definitely something he did not want.

At the same time, he was perceptively aware of what she did want, and was afraid of being trapped.

"I have no intention of marrying anybody!" he told himself firmly as he drove home.

He kissed Maisie's hand when he said goodbye.

She raised her baby face to his.

Something cautious in his mind told him that if he kissed her lips she would take it as being a proposal of marriage.

He was almost relieved the next day to be asked by the Secretary of State for Foreign Affairs to go to Paris.

Because he was extremely clever, Lord Selwyn was often required to step in where the regular Diplomats had failed.

He was invariably successful and was therefore asked again and again to undertake what others had failed to achieve.

Usually the whole thing amused him.

He enjoyed pitting his wits against men who were renowned for their astute brains.

One of his greatest assets was that he spoke most European languages fluently.

He had recently spent some time in Austria, in Rome, and now in Paris.

On each occasion he had returned triumphant, and Lord Clarendon had said:

"I cannot think what I would do without you, Selwyn! I suppose you realise that instead of wasting your time with a lot of brainless women you could be sitting in my chair?"

Lord Selwyn held up his hand in horror.

"God forbid! I have no wish to involve myself in Politics, and I carry out your missions simply because I enjoy them."

Owing to Maisie, he had not enjoyed this last one as much as he had expected.

He was unable to respond to the eroticism that was part of Paris.

He found himself continually thinking that Maisie was pure and untouched.

One day a man would awaken her to the joys of love, but it was obvious she would not wait for ever.

Lord Selwyn was well aware that he had only to say the word and she would be in his arms.

He would be kissing her lips, which he was almost sure had never been kissed.

The question was—could he bring himself to say the magic words that she longed to hear?

"Abracadabra! Will you be my wife!"

It was almost like appearing in a Play where he was cast as the Hero.

But the price he would have to pay for the hand of the Princess was a very high one—his freedom.

Finally he made up his mind.

He had never before met anyone he wanted to marry. Was it possible he would find anybody more suitable?

Of course, he wanted a woman who had never known another man before him.

He could not for a second contemplate marrying a promiscuous woman and have her be the mother of his children.

Selwyn had, in fact, sometimes felt ashamed when he

had made love to another man's wife who had sons and daughters by him.

He did not put it into words, but something idealistic within him felt that she degraded her womanhood.

At the same time, how could he contemplate being married to a *débutante* of eighteen?

She would have been educated by Governesses who knew little more than she did herself.

Maisie had not been able to travel while she tended her sick husband, but at least she could have read books.

He knew the Library at Brambury Hall was very extensive.

"I will take her to the places she has only read about," he told himself. "I will take her to Notre Dame in Paris, the Colosseum in Rome, the Parthenon in Athens, the Pyramids in Egypt."

He was certain, although he had never discussed it with her, that she would appreciate them as much as he did.

Perhaps she would find in all the places, as he had, a deeper meaning which was really spiritual.

It was something the average tourist missed.

Lord Selwyn prided himself that, like the Chinese, he was able to look at the "World Behind the World."

'I will see her to-morrow,' he thought.

It was no use denying the reason for his hurrying.

It was why he had found Paris cold, dull, and a repetition of the obvious.

Why was he restless?

Maisie! Maisie!

He thought he could see her everywhere he looked, hear her voice whenever he listened.

The carriage stopped outside his front-door.

"Thank you for bringing me home," he said to the French Diplomat in his own language. "I am extremely grateful."

"It is always a pleasure to see you, *Monsieur*," the Diplomat replied, "and I am one of your greatest admirers."

Lord Selwyn laughed.

He walked into the house and the Butler looked at him in surprise.

"We weren't expecting Your Lordship back so soon!" he exclaimed.

"I know, Barker," Lord Selwyn answered, "and I did not have time to let Mr. Stevens know. I suppose the Chef can provide me with something to eat?"

"Of course, M'Lord, and it's a pleasure to have Your Lordship back with us."

Lord Selwyn walked into the Library.

Because he liked to have his books around him, he kept his writing-desk at one end of it.

As he expected, the desk was piled with correspondence neatly arranged.

He saw there was a lot of work to be done.

He was debating whether he should visit Maisie to-night or wait until to-morrow.

He decided that it would be a mistake to rush anything.

In any case, she would undoubtedly have a party or some other engagement this evening.

He would only upset her arrangements if he appeared unexpectedly.

"I will send her a note first thing in the morning," he

decided, "asking if we can dine alone. She will know exactly what to expect."

He was thinking what flowers to order to decorate the table when his Secretary, Mr. Stevens, came into the room.

"This is a surprise, My Lord!" he exclaimed.

"I finished what I had to do sooner than I expected," Lord Selwyn explained briefly.

As he spoke, a footman appeared with an open bottle of champagne in a wine-cooler.

He set it down on the grog-table and poured out a glass for Lord Selwyn before he withdrew.

As he sipped it, Lord Selwyn, in his mind, drank a toast to the future.

Then he looked down at his desk.

"I see there is a lot of work for me to do!" he remarked to Mr. Stevens.

His Secretary nodded.

"It is not as bad as it might be, My Lord," he said. "There are a number of invitations, and one from Her Majesty the Queen. Then I must draw your attention to an important letter which needs your immediate response."

Lord Selwyn raised his eye-brows.

"Important?" he asked. "In what way?"

"It concerns your great-uncle, My Lord."

"My great-uncle? Which one?"

"Lord Durham."

Lord Selwyn stared at his Secretary.

"Lord Durham? My father's uncle? I have not thought of him for years! In fact, I thought he was dead."

"No, he has just died, My Lord. He was eighty-nine."

19

"Yes, I suppose he must have been," Lord Selwyn said. "He has been living abroad."

"Yes, My Lord, in Penang."

Lord Selwyn gave an exclamation.

"I remember. He retired from Hong Kong, where he had been the Chief Judge for God knows how many years, but he refused to return to England."

"That is correct, My Lord."

"My father's family considered it an insult that he had no wish to be with us," Lord Selwyn said. "I seem to remember his saying in a letter that he thought of the East as his home and would feel out of place anywhere else."

Mr. Stevens picked up one of the letters from the desk and now he handed it to Lord Selwyn.

He saw it was written from George Town in Penang.

It was obviously from a firm of Solicitors who were both English and Chinese.

He read the letter which informed him that his great-uncle had died and had left him his house and his estate.

He had also left him quite a considerable amount of money.

The letter ended by saying that the Solicitors awaited his instructions.

If it was possible, they would appreciate it if he could come to Penang to see for himself what he had inherited.

Lord Selwyn read the letter and looked at Mr. Stevens.

"Well, that is certainly a surprise!" he exclaimed. "I never expected Great-Uncle Edward to remember me in his Will!"

He laughed ironically before he said:

"God knows what I can do with a Plantation in Pen-ang!"

As he was speaking, he was thinking that Penang was a small island off the Malay Peninsula.

It was a place he had never thought of visiting.

He had been to India, and when he was there had contemplated going on to Singapore.

However, he had come straight home.

There was so much for him to do in England that he could not spare the time to explore any more of the Far East.

"Why did my uncle settle in Penang, of all places?"

He was really thinking out loud, but Mr. Stevens replied:

"I believe it is a beautiful island, My Lord, and very prosperous as a Trading Post."

Lord Selwyn was not listening.

He had put down the letter from the Solicitors.

On the desk beside a pile of invitations there was one letter lying by itself.

For a moment he thought it might be from Maisie.

Mr. Stevens had strict instructions not to open any letter which looked as if it might be private.

He very seldom made a mistake.

Now, as this letter was lying by itself, Lord Selwyn thought it would be from a woman.

When he picked it up he saw that it was not in Maisie's hand-writing.

The envelope was sealed, and because he was curious, he opened it at once.

He was aware that Mr. Stevens was waiting to show him the rest of his mail.

Inside the envelope there was one sheet of writing-paper.

It was of good quality, although not engraved with an address.

Then, as he looked at the hand-writing, he was sure it had come from a woman and wondered who it could be.

Written in a flowing hand, he read:

> *You are being deceived by two*
> *treacherous blue eyes and a lying*
> *tongue. If you wait in the Mews*
> *at the back of a certain house in Grosvenor*
> *Square, and no doubt you will learn a*
> *great deal more than you know already.*
>   *A Friend*

Lord Selwyn stared at the letter in sheer astonishment.

He could not remember ever before receiving an anonymous letter, and certainly not one from a so-called "friend."

It was quite obvious to whom it referred.

He thought angrily that only a woman could attack another in such an underhand and disgusting manner.

"When did this letter arrive?" he asked Mr. Stevens.

"It was not posted, My Lord, but dropped through the letter-box."

Lord Selwyn saw now there was no stamp on the envelope.

He did not speak, and after a moment Mr. Stevens asked:

"Is it anything I should deal with, My Lord?"

"No, no, of course not!"

Lord Selwyn put the letter back into the envelope and placed it in his pocket.

For a moment he hesitated. Then he said:

"I think the rest of the correspondence will have to wait until the morning. I will go up and have my bath."

He walked out of the Library.

Mr. Stevens looked after him with an expression of concern in his eyes.

Something had gone wrong.

Selwyn was not sure what it was, but he was quite certain that the letter had come from a woman.

"It is always a woman who is at the bottom of any trouble!" he said to himself bitterly.

As he spoke he picked up the letter from Penang.

chapter two

LORD Selwyn, having been to see Lord Clarendon about his mission to Paris, returned home.

He had not been in touch with any of his friends.

When he was alone in the Library, he read again the letter he had received from "A Friend."

"I will tear it up and throw it away," he told himself.

He had always despised people who wrote anonymous letters.

He remembered his father saying that the only place for them was the dustbin.

He dined alone because he had no wish for anyone to know he was in London.

Afterwards he felt an irresistible urge to go to the back of Maisie's house.

He could remember her saying in her childlike way:

"It is so disappointing for me that while you have a lovely private garden at the back of your house, I have only the garden of the Square, which everybody uses."

Lord Selwyn had smiled because he rather prided himself on his garden.

The majority of the plants were potted out.

Nevertheless, he managed to grow some delightful

white and purple lilacs, and one bed was devoted entirely to roses.

"When they built Grosvenor Square," Maisie had continued, "they put the Mews behind the houses. As my house is on the East side, I get the morning sun only in the rooms at the back."

"So I expect that is where you sleep," Lord Selwyn remarked.

He thought as he spoke that she reminded him of the Spring sunshine, bringing up the snowdrops and the violets.

Maisie looked at him with her large blue eyes.

"How did you guess that I love the sun?" she asked. "And of course my room is at the back. It is decorated very beautifully and on the First Floor, so it saves me from having to run up a lot of stairs."

She laughed like a child, as if she enjoyed stairs.

Lord Selwyn thought it would be many years before she found them tiresome.

Now, as the conversation came back to him, he was frowning.

Could there really be anything in what the anonymous letter said?

What was it implying?

'I will show it to Maisie to-morrow,' he thought, 'and she will give me an explanation. I will certainly not demean myself by spying on her.'

When dinner was finished, and it had been an excellent one, he settled himself comfortably in an armchair in the Library with a book.

It had just arrived and he was looking forward to reading it.

It was a Biography of the famous Lord Melbourne in whom he had always been very interested.

He knew he would enjoy every word.

An hour later he found he had not turned over more than three pages.

It was impossible to remember even what little he had read.

All he could see was two innocent blue eyes looking up into his and a voice saying with a little sob:

"I have . . . never known . . . love, but . . . perhaps one day I shall . . . find it."

He realised as she spoke that it was his cue to say that he loved her.

The conversation had, however, taken place at a party.

Although they were alone, they were sitting in the Conservatory of their Hostess's house.

If there was one thing Lord Selwyn really disliked, it was drawing attention to himself in public.

He was frightened because Maisie was so young and unsophisticated, that if he spoke to her of love she might throw herself into his arms.

It was what women usually did.

But he had no intention of risking their being interrupted by other members of the party.

They were dancing in a nearby room.

Instead, he said gently:

"That is certainly something we must talk about another time."

Any other woman would have looked up at him.

There would have been an expression in her eyes that told him she understood what he was saying.

And there would have been an obvious invitation in them which he would understand.

Maisie had only looked down shyly, as if she thought she had been indiscreet.

Then she had risen to her feet, saying:

"I am sure we . . . should go . . . back to the Ball-Room."

'She is very young,' Lord Selwyn had thought for the thousandth time.

When he had finally admitted that he loved her, he knew the only thing he could offer her was marriage.

Now he thought that if anyone was slandering Maisie, he would make them pay for it.

It would not be difficult to find out who had written the anonymous letter.

The writer had obviously not attempted to disguise her hand-writing.

He was sure that if he showed the envelope to some of his closest friends, they would know who had addressed it.

He rose to his feet.

"I will go to the Mews behind Maisie's house," he told himself, "and when I find nothing I will somehow contrive to stop this disgraceful insinuation against her virtue."

At a quarter to twelve, wearing his fur-lined coat, he left his house to walk to Grosvenor Square.

It would take him less than five minutes to reach the Mews.

He thought of himself as a Knight in armour going out to defend the woman he loved—a besieged Princess.

"It is obvious," he ruminated, "that because Maisie

28

is so beautiful and so rich there are other women who wish to tear her to pieces.''

His lips tightened.

''Well, I will stop it! If it is the last thing I do, I will prevent this filthy slander from going any further!''

It was certainly something he would not tolerate concerning his wife.

It was, of course, a mistake for Maisie to be in the social position she was without a husband to protect her.

Granted her chaperone, Lady Elton was well-known and respected, but she was old, and could not always accompany Maisie.

Not day after day and night after night, as would be expected of the chaperone to a young girl.

It was quite obvious to Lord Selwyn what could be done about it.

Once he married Maisie there would be no more talk and no more scandal.

It was a bright night and there was magic in the air.

The sky was filled with stars, and there was a half-moon.

There was enough light for him to see his way without any difficulty.

He entered the Mews from the Park side of the Square.

He walked past a number of houses of which he knew the occupants.

As they were mostly elderly, they either did not go out much at night or came home early.

The doors to their stables in the Mews were closed.

There was no sign of any grooms.

Lord Selwyn could hear the movement of the horses in their stalls as he walked past them.

The Mews itself was deserted.

Maisie's house was half-way down the East side of the Square.

It had a very impressive facade with a porticoed front-door.

On the First Floor there was a large Reception Room in which she gave her parties.

He knew the only other room must be her bedroom, of which she had spoken.

On the next floor he knew from experience of other houses there would be several large and high-ceilinged bedrooms.

He suspected that Lady Elton occupied the largest, which would look out over the Square.

When he reached the house he was aware there were stables on both sides of the Mews.

From the side nearest the house he could hear the sound of horses.

On the other side, however, the stables appeared to be unused.

It struck him that if Maisie did not ride in the Park, she would keep only two carriage horses.

They would, therefore, not require so much accommodation.

It was still not yet twelve o'clock and he wondered where he should conceal himself.

On an impulse he tried the side-door of the stable opposite to the one where the horses were.

He found it was unbolted.

He looked inside and saw, as he had suspected, that it was not in use.

There were four stalls, all of them empty.

On one side of the centre door which the horses used there was a window.

It was high up on the wall so that he could look out of it only when he was standing.

On the window-sill there was a woven brush for grooming horses, which had obviously been overlooked.

There was no straw in the stalls and no food in the mangers.

He knew that if he stood where he was, he could watch Maisie's house and not be seen.

He shut the door behind him and moved to the window.

He was telling himself as he did so that he was not spying on her, but protecting her.

Nothing would happen, and he would kill this lie before it went any further.

There was enough light outside for him to see the stable opposite him and the upper windows of the house behind it.

Now he could discern quite clearly the three large high windows of the Drawing-Room on the First Floor.

The curtains were drawn and there was no light coming from there.

Then he looked to the left and could see the window which must belong to Maisie's bedroom.

It was the same shape as those of the Drawing-Room, but there was definitely a light behind its curtains.

He fancied, although he could not be sure, that they were the same colour as Maisie's eyes.

He realised that the stable ended beneath the third Drawing-Room window.

Then he saw attached to it was the Coach-House where Maisie's carriage would be kept.

It was a large building, the front almost completely consisting of double doors, and it had a flat roof.

Lord Selwyn stood looking at it, realising the minutes were ticking by and nothing was happening.

He was cold and beginning to think that the whole thing was a hoax.

Perhaps the anonymous letter had not been written by a woman, but by one of the members of Whites Club who wanted to "pull his leg."

It was a joke that did not amuse him.

At the same time, it was possible that somebody might imagine he was being witty in doing such a thing.

Then suddenly there was the sound—not very loud—of footsteps, and he was aware that somebody was coming down the Mews, not from the direction from which he had come, but from the opposite end, which led into Carlos Place.

Now the footsteps came nearer.

A man passed the window through which Lord Selwyn was looking, and in the moonlight he recognised him at once.

He was a member of his Club.

In fact, Lord Selwyn knew the man quite well, as they frequently attended the same parties.

D'Arcy Claverton was on the list of all the top Hostesses because he made himself so pleasant.

He was a welcome "extra" man at every party and at any dinner where the Guest of Honour failed to turn up at the last moment.

He was also, Lord Selwyn knew, an ardent womaniser.

He spent his life flitting from *Boudoir* to *Boudoir*.

He had no money and therefore had to use his considerable attractions in order to live comfortably and extravagantly.

Lord Selwyn had known him for years.

He neither liked nor disliked D'Arcy Claverton.

He merely accepted him as being part of the world in which he moved.

He was well aware that to all intents and purposes he was a waster, an opportunist.

At the same time, he accepted his position with such good humour that few people bothered to criticise him.

Now, as he passed the window, Lord Selwyn drew in his breath.

What was D'Arcy Claverton doing here?

What reason could he have for visiting the Mews?

The last time he had been in Whites he had been told of an *affaire de coeur* D'Arcy was having with a much-acclaimed Beauty.

She lived in Berkeley Square and had a husband who was an exceedingly wealthy man.

He found, however, that the Social Life bored him.

He therefore spent his time hunting, shooting, and fishing in the proper seasons.

In the meantime, his wife entertained in London.

Berkeley Square was not far away, and that, Lord Selwyn told himself quickly, was where D'Arcy Claverton had just come from.

A split second later D'Arcy paused.

Watching him, Lord Selwyn was aware that by this time he was outside the Coach-House.

He was looking up at the window above him.

Lord Selwyn lowered his head because he was afraid of what he was seeing.

But he could not take his eyes off the man outside.

D'Arcy Claverton moved to a side-door of the Coach-House, which Lord Selwyn had not noticed before.

He disappeared inside, leaving the door open.

A second later he reappeared carrying a short ladder.

He put it against the side of the Coach-House, shut the door, and climbed up.

Lord Selwyn could not believe what he was seeing.

Now D'Arcy was standing on top of the flat roof and he drew the ladder up after him.

He laid it down so that it could not be seen from the Mews.

Then Lord Selwyn saw him step forward to knock gently on the window.

The curtains parted and Maisie—Lord Selwyn could see her quite clearly—came from behind them.

She opened the window.

As she did so, D'Arcy looked up and down the Mews to see if there was anybody in sight.

Reassured, he climbed deftly and swiftly over the window-ledge and into the room.

Lord Selwyn had a glimpse of Maisie moving backwards through the curtains.

D'Arcy followed her and shut the window, and the curtains fell back into place.

It all happened so quickly that Lord Selwyn felt it must be an illusion.

But there was the window which had opened.

Below it, on the flat roof, lay the ladder by which D'Arcy Claverton had entered Maisie's bedroom.

That was the way he would leave.

It was true! True what the anonymous letter had told him.

Lord Selwyn had to admit he had indeed learnt more than he had known before.

He felt the blood throbbing in his temples and his anger rise.

It became a burning fire coursing through his veins.

He wanted to climb into the room himself and tell Maisie exactly what he thought of her.

He clenched his fists, wishing he could thrash D'Arcy Claverton into unconsciousness.

Then he knew he had no one to blame but himself.

He had been fool enough to let another man rob him while he wiffle-waffled instead of sweeping Maisie off her feet.

Then he asked himself if D'Arcy was the first lover she had taken.

There might easily have been others before he met her.

After all, he had not been away in Paris for long.

Was it possible that her wide-eyed, childlike look of innocence and her confession "only to him" was just an act?

Lord Selwyn found it hard to believe.

Yet his intelligence told him that D'Arcy or no D'Arcy, she would still be looking for a husband.

What she wanted was somebody as distinguished as himself.

It was a long time before he moved from the window in the stable.

He let himself out and walked down the Mews and back to his own house in Park Lane.

As he went, all he could think of was Maisie in D'Arcy Claverton's arms.

She would be learning about love from a man who was undoubtedly an expert.

But he was a man she would certainly not marry because he was not important enough.

Lord Selwyn entered his house with an expression on his handsome face which made the night-footman look at him.

It was seldom the Master had one of his "black moods."

When he did, the whole of the household staff shook until it was over.

Lord Selwyn handed the footman his top hat and his cape without saying a word.

He walked to the Library.

He had no wish to go to bed. He wanted to think about what had just occurred.

He felt he needed to adjust himself to a situation that had never happened to him before.

He could never remember any woman in whom he was interested preferring another lover to himself.

She might have a husband, but that was a different matter.

It had always been he who tired first of an affair.

It had been he who said goodbye, he who cleverly— and he was clever—brought a love-affair that was dying to a quick end.

And yet now he had been passed at the winning-post.

He had to admit that while nobody else was aware of it but himself, he had been made to feel a fool.

What he minded more than anything else was that he had been wrong about Maisie.

He had always prided himself on his intuition where people were concerned.

With employees he engaged he had no need of references.

"I can read a man's character myself," he would sometimes say boastingly. "And I am very perceptive about whether he is good or bad."

"Are you telling me," somebody had asked, "that you are never wrong?"

"I cannot remember it ever happening," Lord Selwyn had replied.

He thought he could judge women in the same way.

He had steered clear of several "Sirens" simply because he knew instinctively that they were bad and unpredictable.

Yet Maisie had managed to deceive him.

Maisie, with her innocent blue eyes and soft voice, telling him that she knew nothing about love.

He was unable to sit still in the Library.

He walked up and down the room, raging not at Maisie but himself.

"Why did I not know? Why did I not guess?" he asked.

"How could she make me believe what she wanted me to, and I was unaware it was untrue?"

The revelation seemed to strike at his own character.

He felt as if there were a stranger in his shoes instead of himself.

It was upsetting, disconcerting, and, he thought, humiliating.

There was no use pretending that he had not been abjectly defeated when he was least expecting it, and by D'Arcy Claverton, of all men.

Like a great many before him, Lord Selwyn was prouder of his brain than of his body.

He felt himself superior to most of the men with whom he was in constant touch.

This was simply because he was far more intelligent than they were.

He was also very much more knowledgeable.

Finally—and now he knew it had been stupid of him—he had believed that women also admired him for the same reason.

He admitted bitterly that he had tried to woo Maisie by making her admire him, and he had failed.

He should have kissed her and become her lover.

Instead, he had thought—believing such behaviour would shock her—that he should propose marriage before he even touched her.

"I must have been off my head," he said now.

He walked to the window and pulled back the curtains.

The garden in the moonlight was breathtaking and had an ethereal, mystic look.

Lord Selwyn knew that an hour earlier he would have compared it to Maisie.

He closed the curtains, feeling that the beauty outside only added to his anger and sense of frustration.

"I will go to bed," he decided.

He walked passed his desk.

As he did so, he saw lying on the blotter the letter his Secretary had wanted him to answer.

He had put it on one side because he was thinking

only of the anonymous letter he had received, the letter with its information about Maisie that had proved undoubtedly true.

He thought savagely of what D'Arcy Claverton and Maisie were doing at this moment.

Involuntarily he clenched his fingers together.

Then he realised that he was crushing the letter which had come from Penang.

He thought his Secretary would think it strange if the letter, considering what it contained, was crumpled or torn.

Quickly he put it down on the blotter and tried to press it back into shape.

It was then that the word "Penang" seemed to jump out at him.

It was a small island a long way away.

At the same time, a beautiful one, and with the importance of a Trading Post.

It was as if somebody were speaking to him, telling him about it.

He found himself thinking of moving in a ship down the Mediterranean through the newly opened Suez Canal into the Indian Ocean.

He picked up the letter and read it again.

Then he asked himself—why not?

If he stayed here, he would have to explain to Maisie why he no longer wished to see her.

Apart from Maisie, there was the unknown "Friend" who had sent him the anonymous letter.

She had known, whoever "she" might be, what was happening.

How many other people?

Suddenly it struck him that because he was so important, it had been impossible for him to spend the time he had with Maisie without people talking about it.

Then he had an idea which was horrifying.

Perhaps already bets were being placed in Whites Club as to whether or not she would catch him.

If he dropped her now, there might easily be a number of friends who would guess the reason.

D'Arcy Claverton for sure would guess why he had sheered off.

D'Arcy would talk, and was there ever any gossip that was not known in the Clubs of St. James's?

Everything sensitive in Lord Selwyn shrank from the idea.

He would know, of course, that they were talking about him.

There would be that sudden stare when he came into a room.

There would be an infuriating twinkle in his friends' eyes, or a "knowing" look which he would dislike even more.

There would be laughter and speculation.

Women would search for every little piece of information to add to what they already knew.

Suddenly he felt he could not bear it and certainly could not face it.

And why should he?

There was an escape from it right in front of him and he would be a fool to ignore it.

That he had been left a fortune and an estate in a distant part of the world was something to be talked about, something to envy.

"Money always goes to money!" his friends would say.

"It *would* be Selwyn, the lucky devil!"

"I wish somebody would leave *me* a fortune!"

"He can hardly want to live in Penang!"

"One never knows! He might find it a comfortable nest with one of his love-birds!"

He could hear the voices, the laughter, the double entendres, and occasionally a touch of malice.

"I would be a fool not to take what the gods have offered me!"

He put the letter from the Solicitors back on his desk and slowly went upstairs to his bedroom.

His valet was already there waiting for him.

He suspected that Higgins, who was always bright and cheerful whatever time he arrived upstairs, had an arrangement with the night-footmen.

He could sleep until his Master came in through the front-door, when they would wake him.

Lord Selwyn let the man help him undress, but did not speak until he was ready for bed.

Then he said in his ordinary voice:

"Start packing first thing in the morning, Higgins. We will be leaving for Penang either to-morrow or first thing the following day. It is near the Equator."

There was a second's silence.

Then Higgins replied in the same indifferent manner that his Master had spoken:

"Will it be formal or informal, M'Lord?"

"Better be prepared for both," Lord Selwyn replied.

"Very good, M'Lord."

Higgins walked towards the door, and Lord Selwyn was sure that he was grinning.

He knew that Higgins enjoyed the unexpected more than anything else.

They would be going away from what he described as the "humdrum."

They had only just come back from Paris, and now they were leaving again.

'Leaving' Lord Selwyn thought savagely, not only unexpectedly, but also ignominiously.

Then he laughed.

"I always knew it would be a mistake for me to marry!" he told himself defiantly.

But for the moment he knew that his relief was bittersweet, and because of Maisie, for the moment he hated women.

They were—all of them—as the anonymous note had told him, treacherous!

*   *   *

The next morning anybody who knew Lord Selwyn well would have realised that he had withdrawn into himself.

There was a grim expression on his face which was also cynical.

It made him look older than his years.

He broke the news to Mr. Stevens that he intended to go at once to Penang.

He was glad to find there was a P & O Liner leaving Tilbury Dock for Calcutta at mid-night.

It was one of the largest, and certainly the most comfortable of the East-bound ships.

Mr. Stevens put the wheels in motion for his Master to have the best accommodation possible.

In the meantime, Lord Selwyn ploughed through the large pile of correspondence on his desk.

He deliberately refrained from going anywhere where he would see his close friends.

They might communicate his whereabouts to Maisie.

The only person he did see during the afternoon was his mother's remaining sister.

She lived very quietly in a small house in Belgravia.

He told her of the death of her uncle, Lord Durham, and that he had been left all his money and an estate and plantation in Penang.

His aunt, who was a widow, was delighted.

"Edward was always an extremely clever man," she said, "but he never married, and we heard about his success in Hong Kong only when he wrote to us each Christmas."

Lord Selwyn laughed.

"Is that the only communication you had with him?"

"I believe he preferred your mother to the rest of the family," his aunt replied, "which is the reason why he made you his heir."

"Of course I am very grateful," Lord Selwyn said, "and I think the least I can do is to inspect the property, as the Solicitors have begged me to do."

"Of course you must!" his aunt said. "I only wish I were young enough to come with you."

"I shall not be away for long," Lord Selwyn answered, "and I will, of course, report to you exactly what has been happening when I return."

"I expect you know that Edward had very good taste,"

his aunt said, "and I imagine that over the years he has collected a lot of Chinese jade and porcelain which would certainly be acceptable at Wyn Hall."

Lord Selwyn laughed.

"I only hope there is room for it," he said.

He paused and then continued:

"I was thinking only the other day that we have so many treasures that if we have any more, we shall have to build an extension to the house!"

His aunt gave a cry.

"Do be careful not to spoil the perfection of the architecture. At the same time, what is more important than treasures is that you should have children to inherit them!"

Lord Selwyn frowned, although she did not notice it.

"You know we are all longing for you to have a son, and your mother was always desperately disappointed that you were an only child."

Lord Selwyn rose to his feet.

"As I am leaving in a few hours for Tilbury," he said, "I think I should be getting back. But I felt you were the one person who would be interested in hearing what Great-Uncle Edward has left me."

"Bring me back a souvenir from Penang," his aunt begged, "and take care of yourself. I believe, despite the efforts of the British Navy, there are still pirates in that part of the world and some very unpleasant murders take place there."

"Now you are trying to frighten me!" Lord Selwyn protested. "But I promise I will take very great care of myself, and I will not forget to bring you something really beautiful from Penang."

He kissed his aunt goodbye, and drove back to Park Lane.

Now he felt he had "cleared the decks" and could set off into the unknown without any further preparations.

He knew that his aunt, although she was his mother's sister, was closely in touch with his father's relations.

They would, therefore, be informed by her of where he had gone.

He knew that quite a number of them would expect a present now that he had come into more money.

He made a mental note to tell Mr. Stevens to send his aunts on both sides of the family either flowers or a case of champagne.

When he arrived back at Park Lane, Barker the Butler said to him as he came through the door:

"There's a Lady waiting to see you, M'Lord."

Lord Selwyn stiffened.

"A Lady?" he questioned.

"Lady Brambury, M'Lord. She arrived half-an-hour ago, and is waiting for your Lordship's return."

Lord Selwyn drew in his breath.

For a moment he contemplated telling Barker to say that he would not be back until late in the evening.

Then he told himself that he would be damned if he would run away from anybody—even Maisie.

"Her Ladyship's in the Drawing-Room, M'Lord," Barker said.

He walked ahead of Lord Selwyn as he spoke, and the latter could do nothing but follow him.

Barker opened the door and he walked in.

Maisie was standing at the window, looking out into the sunlit garden.

He appreciated—and the knowledge made him tighten his lips—that she was looking very lovely.

At the same time, her whole attire made her look young, childlike, and innocent.

As he walked towards her, her blue eyes seemed to light up.

She waited for him, the sunlight on her face.

"You are back!"

It was the soft cooing of a dove.

"Yes, I am back!" Lord Selwyn said. "But I am afraid I am leaving again almost immediately."

Maisie drew in her breath.

"You are . . . going away again?"

She sounded genuinely upset.

"Yes, I am leaving for Penang to-night. My great-uncle has died and left me a house and a Plantation which I must inspect."

Maisie looked up at him.

"Oh . . . then I shall . . . not see . . . you!"

She looked away from him in the manner by which he had been deceived before into thinking she was shy.

There was silence until she asked:

"How . . . how long . . . will you be . . . away?"

"I have no idea," Lord Selwyn replied. "Perhaps a month or more."

"I . . . I shall . . . miss you."

Now she was looking at him again and he could almost swear there were tears in her eyes.

"I have no doubt there will be plenty of people willing to entertain you in my absence!" Lord Selwyn said.

He could not suppress, however hard he tried, a touch of both sarcasm and mockery in the way he spoke.

"It will not be the . . . same without you!" Maisie said forlornly.

He had the sudden feeling she was going to suggest she should go with him.

It was so strong that he knew he was not mistaken.

If he was to save himself from being unpleasant, he would have to act quickly.

He turned and walked across the room to ring the bell.

"What you must do," he said when he was some distance from her, "is to wish me luck and, of course, a safe return."

While he was still speaking the door opened.

"A bottle of champagne, Barker," Lord Selwyn said.

"Very good, M'Lord."

The door shut, and Maisie did not move from the window.

Slowly Lord Selwyn walked a little way towards her, but not too far.

"I wonder if you have ever heard of Penang," he said conversationally. "I believe it is a very attractive island, and, of course, I can always stop at Calcutta on my way home. Lord Mayo, the new Viceroy, is an old friend of mine."

The door opened.

Barker, who always had champagne on hand in case it was required, brought it in on a tray in a silver ice-bucket.

He poured out two glasses and proffered one to Maisie.

She accepted it, and as Lord Selwyn took his he raised it.

"Let us drink first to you and your happiness!" he said.

It was obviously with difficulty that Maisie found her voice.

"To your . . . journey!" she said. "And may you come . . . home very . . . quickly!"

The way she looked at him, Lord Selwyn knew exactly what she meant.

It flashed through his mind that he should tell her the truth—or at least part of it, that he had intended to call on her last night but thought it was too late.

He had walked back through the Mews and had seen something very strange happening, which had made him suspect she was being burgled.

Then he told himself that he would not sink so low.

It would be humiliating to reveal to her that he knew what had taken place between her and D'Arcy Claverton.

"Thank you!" he said aloud. "I am sure your toast will bring me luck and that I shall be quite safe during what will be a long and arduous voyage."

He glanced at the clock, then put down his glass.

"I know you will forgive me," he said, "but I have a thousand things to do before I actually leave, and very little time in which to do them."

"Yes . . . yes . . . of course," Maisie replied, "and . . . please . . . be very careful with . . . yourself. Remember you are . . . wanted in . . . England."

She put out her hand towards him as she spoke, but he appeared not to notice it.

Instead, he walked across the room to the door and she followed him.

They crossed the hall side by side with Barker and two footmen within ear-shot.

Lord Selwyn took Maisie's hand in farewell.

He was aware that her fingers were saying what her lips could not.

Her blue eyes were looking into his, but he looked away to where her carriage was waiting.

As she drove away, he went quickly across the hall and into the Library.

Only when he reached it was he aware that strangely enough, he was no longer angry.

He was no longer steaming inside with the fury of how she had deceived him.

Instead, he knew he had escaped from the clutches of one of the cleverest actresses he had ever seen.

Her performance was quite perfect.

Had it not been for an anonymous letter, he would never have suspected that she was anything other than she pretended to be.

" 'A friend in need is a friend indeed!' " he told himself.

He managed when he had spoken aloud to laugh almost naturally.

chapter three

ANONA walked from the garden into the house.

She was carrying in her arms a huge bunch of orchids that grew so profusely everywhere.

When she had first come to Malaysia she could not believe anything could be more lovely than both the wild and the cultured orchids.

"They are so beautiful, Mama," she said, "that I think even the angels in Heaven must be jealous!"

Her mother had laughed.

She, too, was thrilled with the house that her husband had built for them.

It was on the coast, about four miles from Singapore.

Their neighbours were the Malayans, who lived in tree-like houses.

Their children spent the day splashing in the smooth sea as it lapped on the golden sand.

They had been very happy until Anona's mother died.

For a long time she found it hurt her to go into the garden because it reminded her so vividly of her mother's love of it.

It was her mother who taught her to appreciate all the flora and fauna of the country.

"Just think, darling," she had said, "there are one-hundred-and-fifty different palms!"

"I do not believe it!" Anona exclaimed.

When she began to count the ones they had had in and around the garden, she found her mother was right.

Coconut, sugar, mint, loutan, and areca palms were there in profusion.

She found it hard to appreciate them, even when they were in bloom, when she could see the orchids.

The butterflies fluttered around them.

She would believe she was back in her childhood, when she thought the butterflies were fairies.

Pink, orange, vermillion, yellow, and turquoise, they seemed almost part of the flowers.

The two together made her certain that she was living in a Heaven on Earth.

After her mother died, her father arranged that she should be looked after by a kind, elderly woman.

She had been living in a small house in Singapore with her married daughter.

She had been delighted to come to live in the attractive house with its Chinese green tiled roof and its large, comfortable rooms.

In them there was an amazing amount of treasures.

Captain Guy Ranson, she thought, had excellent taste.

But it was his daughter who appreciated the exquisite pieces of jade, pink quartz and crystal which he brought back with him.

First he had brought them as gifts for his wife, then for Anona.

Having originally been in the Royal Navy, Captain Ranson had transferred to the East India Company.

He had been for several years in command of various of their cargo-boats.

There was an enormous amount of trading going on at that time in the Singapore area.

Yet recently Anona found he came home much more frequently than he had in the past.

She never knew when to expect him.

Suddenly she would hear his voice calling her and she would run from the garden or down the stairs to greet him.

"You are home! You are home, Papa!" she would cry. "How wonderful! I thought it would be weeks before I would see you again!"

"I missed you, my Poppet," he would say. "What have you been doing with yourself?"

It was difficult to make her quiet life sound interesting. Anona longed to hear what he had been doing.

She found, however, that her father disliked talking about himself.

"When I am working I concentrate on my work," he said. "When I come home I want to hear about you."

Because very little happened in the house amongst the palm trees, to please him Anona read everything she could.

He had ordered innumerable books from Singapore.

He even insisted that every new book that came into the Library should be sent to Anona.

She knew he himself had little time to read.

She would therefore describe to him the plots and paint a picture in words of the background of the book.

If it was at all controversial, she would duel with her

father in argument as to whether the action described was right or wrong.

She had in the last two or three months concentrated on Political and Historical books.

She found that her father was very knowledgeable on both subjects, especially where it concerned the Far East, where they lived.

They would talk about India, Burma, and, of course, China.

This was an enigmatic country, but then, they knew a great number of Chinese people.

Singapore was full of them, and Anona never stopped being intrigued and amused by their many traditional ceremonies and customs.

Her father had explained to her a great deal about the Chinese people.

Their belief in their gods, their ancestry, worship, and their capacity for looking into the "World Beyond the World."

To illustrate what he told her, the next time he came home he had brought her two very old and, she was sure, very valuable Chinese pictures.

They were hung on the Sitting-Room wall.

Anona would often sit, contemplating them and trying to understand what the artist had portrayed.

She knew they had a spiritual meaning.

The exquisitely drawn clouds which lay above the flowers and streams were the "Ceiling of Ordinary Life."

That was the day-to-day world in which she lived.

The white peaks above the clouds, vivid against the sky, meant something very different.

She was not certain what it was.

'Perhaps one day I shall find out for myself,' she thought a little wistfully.

At the same time, she wished her father were there to help her.

She did not allow the Malayan servants to dust the exquisite pieces of jade.

Her mother had arranged them in the Sitting-Room on special shelves.

They had been added to considerably since her death.

When Anona touched any of the pieces of jade, which was as green as the sea, she would remember that jade expelled evil thoughts from the mind.

"How could I have any evil thoughts in this beautiful place?" she asked herself.

But to make certain, she stroked the jade carefully.

Then she recalled that the Chinese also believed it was charged with a creative force.

"Have I any?" she enquired of herself.

She thought it was what her father had, and it enveloped him like an aura.

She could feel that everybody with whom he came in contact felt the same.

"Everyone who served with you in your ships, Papa, must love you very much," she said to him once.

"Why do you think that?" he asked.

"Because it is not only what you say, or what you do—and you know how kind you are—it is that you give out something towards them, something they can feel, like a ray of sunshine."

Her father had smiled.

"Thank you, my dear, but sometimes, when I am

angry, it must be like a flash of fork-lightning. Then people are afraid.''

Anona had laughed and flung her arms round his neck.

"No one could be afraid of you, Papa, and I love you!"

"I love you too, my Poppet," he said. "That is why I work so hard to make sure you are always safe."

She looked at him in surprise.

"I am quite safe here with Chang to look after me, and all his family."

The Malayan servants had a small bamboo hut down on the edge of the sea.

They all worked with their father in the house and the garden.

Anona thought it would be impossible to feel lonely or neglected when they were there.

Even the smallest child, who was only three years old, would sit on the grass, picking out the weeds.

He would look so adorable as he did so that it was difficult for Anona not to pick him up as if he were a doll.

Now she carried in the orchids past him.

She went to put them into the tall glass vases which her mother had bought in Singapore.

They would bring a brilliant touch of colour to the Sitting-Room.

She had almost reached the house when she stopped.

She thought she had heard her father calling to her.

Then she was certain she must be mistaken.

He had been home for a week, but he had left again only four days ago.

She heard his voice again.

"Anona! Anona!"

"Papa!" she exclaimed now in sheer astonishment.

She ran into the house through the open French window, putting her orchids down on the nearest table.

She ran on to the front of the house from which his voice had come.

She was right. He was standing just inside the open door.

He was looking very large and handsome.

Because it was so hot, he had taken off his jacket.

As she came to the hall he threw his cap onto a chair and held out his arms.

"Papa, you are back! I can hardly believe you are back!" she said when she could speak.

"I have come back," her father answered in a rather strange voice, "because I have something very important to tell you. Where is Mrs. Boynton?"

"She is not here, Papa."

"Why not?" her father asked.

"The day after you left, a messenger came from Singapore to tell her that her daughter was having her baby sooner than she expected."

"So you are alone!"

"I am perfectly safe, Papa!" Anona said quickly, knowing he disapproved. "Chang is sleeping in the house while she is away, and, of course, his wife and his children are here all day."

She thought her father was going to argue that it was a mistake.

Instead, he said as if he spoke to himself:

"Well, that makes things easier."

She looked at him in surprise, but he did not explain. He merely said:

"I have had nothing to eat since mid-day yesterday. Tell Chang to bring me some food."

"Yes, of course, Papa, but why have you gone hungry?"

Her father did not answer.

Because she knew she must obey his orders, Anona ran into the kitchen. Chang, as she expected, was washing up the plates she had used at breakfast.

"The Master is home, Chang," she said, "and he is very hungry. Please bring him something to eat straight away."

"Master-back?" Chang said in his lilting, sing-song voice. "That good! Bring food quick-quick!"

"That is what he wants." Anona smiled and ran back to her father.

He was in the Sitting-Room, standing, looking out into the garden.

She went up to him and slipped her hand into his.

"What is wrong, Papa? I know you are worried."

"Very worried, my precious," he replied, "and I will tell you about it when Chang has brought me something to eat."

"He is preparing one of your favourite dishes immediately," Anona answered, "and I expect you would like a drink?"

"Yes—of course!" her father said as if he had not thought of it before.

She found the key of a beautiful Chinese lacquer cabinet, where her father locked up his drinks when he went away.

Her mother had never drunk anything alcoholic.

Anona had been considered too young until this year, when she became eighteen.

However, she preferred the delicious juices which Chang made from the fruit which grew wild all round them.

As soon as she had opened the cupboard her father walked to it.

She noticed he poured himself out a much larger amount of brandy than he usually drank.

Now she was aware that he was worried and upset about something.

She knew this not only from his expression but also because she was perceptively aware of his feelings.

She wondered what it could be and only hoped it was not money.

She remembered a period in her parents' life when they were building the house, and money was a critical problem.

"We must economise," her mother used to say helplessly.

The crisis, if that was what it was, had passed.

Then there seemed to be a lot of money, so much, in fact, that Anona was astonished at the things her father acquired first for her mother, then for her.

They included many luxuries that were added to the house.

Because she was rather frightened Anona said a little prayer:

"Please, God ... do not let ... this be serious ... please, God!"

She was too tactful to ask questions.

Yet every time she looked at her father she felt more and more curious.

They had not long to wait before Chang came to say:

"Meal leady, an' hope Master find velly good!"

"I am sure I shall!" Captain Ranson said, rising to his feet.

He walked into the small Dining-Room.

It might have come from any house in Great Britain or any British colony.

There was a polished table in the centre of it, a matching set of chairs, and a sideboard.

Because he knew his wife would appreciate it, there was an exquisite crystal chandelier.

It rivalled those in the Governor's house in Singapore.

Captain Ranson sat down at the table and ate quickly, almost as if he were not tasting the food.

There was fresh fish caught in the sea that morning.

It was covered with the Sweet and Sour Sauces beloved of the Chinese.

There was a salad to go with it, and afterwards Chang brought in a pudding.

It was a mixture of fruit sprinkled with grated coconut and a touch of nutmeg.

Chang was a very skilful Cook.

Anona thought her father looked a little less worried now that he had eaten.

He did not speak until he had finished his meal.

Then he looked at the Grandfather Clock which stood in one corner of the room and had been brought from England.

Rising to his feet, he said:

"Let us go into the Sitting-Room, dearest, and we must not be disturbed!"

Anona looked at him in surprise.

"There is no one here except Chang, and it is very unlikely there will be any callers."

Their closest neighbours lived some way away.

At this time of the morning they would be busy in their mangroves or plantations.

It was only in the evening they were likely to drop in, if her father was at home.

Since Mrs. Boynton had been with her, some women called, but their visits had become few and far between.

Anona followed her father into the Sitting-Room, and he shut the door behind her.

That was unusual in itself.

To keep the house cool they left the doors and windows open.

What movement of air there was at the hottest time of the day could blow through it.

Her father sat down on the sofa and she crossed the room to sit down beside him.

"What is worrying you, Papa?" she asked.

Her father looked away from her.

There was a long pause, as if he were feeling for words.

Then he said:

"Something disastrous has happened, and because it concerns you, my darling, I have to tell you the truth."

"The . . . truth, Papa? What about?"

Again her father seemed to hesitate before he said:

"For the last three years your mother and you believed I was trading in my own ship."

"Yes, of course, Papa. That is what you told us you were doing, and you were lucky to have such valuable cargos."

Her father made a sound that was almost a groan before he said:

"Actually that was a lie!"

Anona looked at him in astonishment.

"A . . . lie . . . Papa?"

"It is true that I had my own ship," Captain Ranson said, "a very fast and up-to-date one, but it was small and I carried no cargo."

Anona stared at him.

"Then . . . what did you . . . do, Papa?"

Her father drew in his breath, then turned his head to look at her.

"This will shock you," he said. "I was a Pirate!"

For a moment Anona felt she could not have heard him aright.

"A . . . a Pirate?" she asked in astonishment. "What do you mean . . . what can . . . you mean?"

"I mean exactly what I say," her father replied. "I was a Pirate, and I preyed on other ships!"

Anona was speechless.

Then she remembered all that she had heard about the Pirates in this area of the World!

She gave a sudden cry of horror.

"You are not . . . a *Prahu*?" she asked incredulously.

She knew that the *Prahu*s were the most deadly, cruel, and terrifying Pirates that sailed the seas round Malaysia.

They were known for their ferocious appearance, having long hair, which they left loose in battle to make themselves look even more frightening.

They were known to board a ship so silently that no one heard their approach.

Then when they had crept on board they would brutally massacre the passengers and crew.

Afterwards they would leave as swiftly and silently as they had come in their specially built boats.

Was it possible—could she really believe that her father was one of them?

"No, of course I am not a *Prahu*!" her father said sharply.

Anona was so relieved that she felt suddenly limp.

"I suppose," her father said quickly, as if he must dispel the horror she felt, "that I have been more of a Highwayman than a *Prahu*."

There was a slight twist to his lips as he added:

"But instead of riding a horse I sailed in a ship, and what I have been doing is much the same as making my victims 'stand and deliver'!"

In a voice that hardly sounded like her own, Anona said:

"Explain . . . to me, Papa."

Because she was frightened, she slipped her hand into his.

His fingers closed over hers so tightly that he almost drained the blood from them.

"I swear to you one thing," he said, "I have never killed anybody."

He was aware that Anona was looking at him as she listened with a look of horror on her face.

"What I did," he said after a moment, "was to board a ship filled with cargo when it was in a secluded bay or anchored for the night, and demand a ransom."

"I . . . I do not . . . understand, Papa."

"I had two of my friends with me," Captain Ranson went on, "who were as poor as I was. We were getting what we thought was a very small salary from the East India Company."

He paused and then continued:

"They were not over-generous towards their Officers, so we concocted this idea between us."

"Tell me . . . so that I . . . understand," Anona pleaded.

The look of horror had left her eyes.

"That is what I am trying to do," her father replied. "I am only thankful, as you will understand, that I do not have to confess this to your mother, for she would have been deeply shocked!"

"As . . . I am . . . Papa!" Anona said without thinking.

She saw the expression of pain on her father's face and wished she had not spoken.

As if to comfort him, she moved a little closer to his side and rested her head against his shoulder.

He put his arm around her.

"What happened," he went on, "was that we bought a very fast boat which, of course, we had to pay for with our first takings."

He looked ahead of him as he spoke, as if he were trying to remember exactly how it had all happened.

"With our first two or three hold-ups, we paid for the ship, and we knew we were onto a good thing!"

"Tell me . . . exactly what . . . you did, Papa," Anona begged.

"We usually chose a Dutch cargo vessel. The Dutch

are not quick-brained, so we were not shot down before we explained what we wanted.''

''Th-they . . . might have . . . killed you, Papa!''

''There was always that risk, but usually we climbed aboard at a time when they were relaxed and had been drinking.''

There was a faint smile on Captain Ranson's lips as he added:

''When we told them what we wanted, they were completely astonished.''

''You . . . demanded money?'' Anona questioned, trying to understand.

''We demanded money in return for leaving their ship immediately and not damaging or stealing their cargo.''

''Why should you . . . do that, Papa?''

''It was something we had no wish to do,'' he replied. ''It was merely a threat. They knew that if they refused, they would risk losing the cargo. They would waste a great deal of time in going back to where they had come from.''

''I . . . think I understand,'' Anona said. ''Go on!''

''It is quite simple,'' her father replied. ''They paid up and, when we had left, it was usually without recriminations and, most important, without a shot being fired or anyone being hurt.''

''I am . . . glad about . . . that,'' Anona said almost beneath her breath.

''So was I,'' her father agreed, ''and because it all seemed so easy, I thought my Highwayman act could go on for ever.''

''Now I understand how it was you could buy so . . .

65

many treasures," Anona said, "and give . . . Mama and . . . me so many . . . presents."

"Do you think I did this entirely for myself!" her father said angrily. "I did it for your mother and you because I loved you both and wanted you to have the best of everything."

Anona put up her hand to touch his cheek.

"As we love . . . you . . . Papa, and you know . . . Mama, until she . . . died, was very . . . very . . . happy."

Her father bowed his head before he went on:

"Then the day before yesterday we boarded a Dutch cargo-boat on its way to Singapore."

There was silence until Anona could not help asking:

"W-what . . . happened, Papa?"

"There was an Englishman aboard," Captain Ranson replied.

"An . . . Englishman?"

"Yes. He had been in the Navy like myself. We had served together for a short time in the same ship, and I am sure he recognised me."

"Oh . . . no . . . Papa . . . !"

"Of course, we always boarded these ships disguised with black faces, and the two men with me wore masks."

"Masks!" Anona murmured.

"I always refused to wear one," her father said, "because I was afraid they would frighten our victims too much, and too quickly."

Anona thought this was sensible, but she did not say so.

"My friends wore masks, but it would have been almost impossible for Harrison, that is the man's name, not to know who I was."

"And you think afterwards he was . . . convinced that you were who you are?" Anona enquired.

"I can only hope he was uncertain," her father replied. "I spoke in a rather different way from the way I usually do, and I ignored him completely."

"But . . . you still took . . . a ransom?"

"I took a ransom and left, but you realise, my darling, what has happened?"

"You . . . think the . . . Englishman will . . . denounce . . . you," Anona whispered.

"I am afraid so, which means I have to go into hiding."

"Oh, Papa, if they . . . catch you . . . what will . . . they do?"

Her father's lips tightened for a moment.

"You know the answer to that."

Anona gave a cry.

How could she not know that Pirates were hanged?

And there was no question of their being reprieved.

She put her arm round her father's neck and clung to him.

"Oh . . . no . . . no . . . Papa! That cannot . . . happen to . . . you! It must . . . not!"

"I agree with you," Captain Ranson said quietly. "It must not happen, not so much for my sake, my Poppet, as for yours!"

Anona had hidden her face against him to hide her tears.

Now she looked up at him in surprise.

"For . . . me? What have . . . I to do . . . with it?"

"Everything!" her father said.

He put his arms round her and held her so close that she could hardly breathe.

"Do you really think I would leave you to face enquiries about me, or allow you to be branded as the daughter of a Pirate?"

Anona could not reply.

Her father, holding her tighter still, said passionately:

"I love you, my precious little daughter, I love you, and if I am to die, I will die as a gentleman and not at the hands of the hangman!"

"Oh . . . please . . . Papa . . . do not . . . d-die!" Anona sobbed.

Now the tears were pouring down her cheeks, and once again she hid her face against her father's neck.

For a moment she felt he was fighting for control.

Then he said:

"Now, listen, my little one, because we have not much time, and a great deal to do."

With a superhuman effort Anona checked her tears.

"W-what do you . . . want me to . . . do, Papa?"

He raised her face to his and very gently wiped away the tears from her eyes and cheeks with his handkerchief.

Then he answered:

"I have thought out a plan which I think will save us both."

"Save . . . you, Papa?"

"Yes, my dearest. At any rate, no one will find me until the trouble blows over."

She had a feeling he was speaking with deliberate optimism.

At the same time, she listened.

"Now, what we are going to do," he said, "is to

leave here at once, telling Chang I am taking you on a visit to stay with some friends. If there are enquiries about me, that is all he will know.''

"But . . . where are we . . . really going . . . Papa?''

"I am taking you to Penang.''

"Penang?'' Anona repeated.

She remembered as she spoke that it was a small island off the north-west coast of Malaysia.

She had heard her father speak of it as a Trading Post, but otherwise she knew nothing about it.

"There is somebody there who I know will look after you,'' her father went on, "but you will realise, my precious, he must not know who you are.''

Anona looked at her father wide-eyed.

"Do . . . you mean . . . I have to . . . pretend to be . . . somebody else?''

"You have to pretend nothing!'' her father answered.

Unexpectedly he took his arm from her and rose to his feet.

Anona was staring at him as he walked across the room.

Then he walked back again, and it was as if he were trying to think clearly.

"I have been working it out all the time I have been travelling home,'' he said at last. "You have to be very brave, and at the same time do exactly as I tell you.''

Because Anona knew her father was afraid she would refuse, she said quickly:

"Of course, Papa. I will do . . . anything you . . . want me to . . . do.''

"Very well,'' he said. "Now listen to what I have planned.''

69

Anona sat on the edge of the sofa and gripped her fingers together.

It was as if she had suddenly been turned out of the Heaven in which she believed she lived.

The Heaven of Happiness which the little house had always been to her had suddenly become a nightmare.

"I am going to take you at once as swiftly as my ship will carry us to Penang," her father said.

He looked at her lovingly before continuing:

"At dawn tomorrow I shall put you in a boat and make sure that you land on the beach owned by a Chinese called Lin Kuan Teng."

Anona put her fingers to her lips and stifled a cry of sheer horror at her father's words.

"He is very rich and very kind, and will," Captain Ranson said, "look after you, especially when he realises that you have lost your memory."

"I have . . . lost . . . my . . . memory?" Anona repeated in a whisper he could hardly hear.

"You remember nothing!" her father said firmly. "Until much later you think that Pirates boarded a ship in which you were travelling, although you cannot remember where."

He paused, then he continued:

"Then someone, and you have no idea who it was, must have rescued you by putting you in the boat that landed up on Mr. Lin Kuan Teng's beach."

Captain Ranson stopped walking up and down to look at his daughter.

As he did so he thought that no one could look more lovely.

She had fair hair like his own, her mother's aristocratic nose, and deep blue eyes.

They were the colour not of the sky, but of a turbulent sea.

She had, too, he knew, a spiritual beauty that was unusual.

It had nothing in common with the pink-and-white prettiness that was characteristically English.

Perhaps because she had lived so long in the East, Anona had the grace of the Malaysian women and the intelligence of the Chinese.

He knew that no man could look at her without drawing in his breath.

He knew he had found a treasure that was so perfect it could not be human.

"That is what I have planned," he said aloud in a hard voice because he was afraid of her reaction.

Anona did not speak, and after a moment he went on:

"You will not only be safe, my Poppet, but you will be helping me. I have to hide, which you know I could not if I take you with me."

He gave a short laugh without any humour in it as he said:

"Can you imagine, if I were accompanied by a very beautiful young woman, what they would say? How they would talk? And the hounds on my heels would find it very easy to find me."

"I . . . I understand . . . Papa," Anona faltered, "and I will . . . do as you . . . tell me . . . but I will be . . . very . . . very frightened!"

"I can understand that," her father said. "At the same

time, I promise you that my Chinese friend is a very kind man with a delightful family.''

He paused a moment before he went on:

"He is of great importance in Penang, and I can think of no one who would look after you better!''

"I . . . I . . . remember . . . nothing!'' Anona said as if she were rehearsing it to herself.

"You can think you were struck on the head, but you are not certain,'' her father said. ''All you know—but not at once, mind—is that your name is Anona.''

Then in a more brisk tone he said:

"When we go abroad I will explain to you that thanks to my activities, of which of course you disapprove, you will, one day, if you need, be able to put your hands on a lot of money.''

"How . . . is that . . . possible?'' Anona enquired.

"I have put into a Bank Account in Singapore a large amount of money in your mother's maiden name.''

He smiled at her, then said:

"You will also find some in a bank in Jakarta, and more in Bangkok.''

He saw she was listening, and he went on:

"Of course, you may not be able to collect it for some time, but when you do, you will at least be provided for as long as you live.''

"I am not . . . interested in . . . m-money, Papa,'' Anona said. ''I just . . . want you to be . . . alive . . . and with me.''

"That is what I want myself,'' her father answered, ''but it all depends on whether or not Harrison denounces me to the authorities.''

He stopped for a moment and then went on:

"That, of course, will mean that the British Navy will be looking for me as well as every cargo-ship afloat."

Anona gave a little cry and jumped up.

She ran to her father and put her arms around him.

"I will be . . . praying . . . praying that . . . you will be . . . safe . . . and I am sure . . . Papa . . . wherever she is . . . Mama will be looking after you and . . . trying to save you."

"I want to believe that," her father said quietly, "and now, my darling, we must go as quickly as possible."

Anona made a helpless little gesture with her hands.

"What . . . am I to . . . take with me?"

"What you have on," her father replied, "and your smartest and most elaborate evening-gown."

He gave an exclamation.

"No! Your mother's! The one she wore when we went to the Ball in Singapore, where she was undoubtedly the most beautiful woman present."

"I-is that what I am to . . . wear in the boat?" Anona asked.

"Yes," her father said. "You will also wear your mother's jewellery."

Anona looked at him in surprise, and he said:

"First, because it will ensure that you are treated with respect, and not just as a castaway, and second, because it will make the story of the 'girl who was washed ashore' more exciting.

He paused, then said more slowly:

"You will be treated, I can only hope and pray, as if you were a Princess."

"Then . . . when I *am* able to . . . remember who I am, people will be . . . disappointed!"

Her father laughed.

Then he said seriously:

"You remember nothing until I allow you to do so."

He stopped for a moment and then continued:

"I will either come back for you, or I will send word that all is well, and the 'bloodhounds' are no longer on my heels."

"Oh . . . Papa . . . be careful!" Anona said. "Be careful . . . I cannot . . . lose you."

"I promise you I will do my best to remain alive," her father answered, "and make no mistake, every second, every minute we stay here is dangerous."

"I will go to get ready," Anona said quietly. "You speak to Chang while I find Mama's gown and her jewellery."

"I will find that," her father replied. "Just pack the things that you will want until we reach Penang."

As he spoke, he walked out of the Sitting-Room towards the kitchen.

Anona watched him go.

Then she realised that he had said he was in danger.

She glanced outside through the open door at the sea, smooth and golden in the sunlight.

She could hear the voice of children laughing on the beach.

The birds were singing in the trees and the butterflies were fluttering over the orchids.

How could it be true?

How could it possibly be true that these terrible things had happened to her father and she was to lose him and everything that was familiar?

Then she told herself she was being selfish.

The only thing that mattered was that he should be safe, that he must not be caught.

She ran up the stairs.

Only when she reached her mother's bedroom did she say frantically as she opened the wardrobe-door:

"Help me . . . Mama! Help me . . . and save Papa. I am frightened . . . so terribly . . . terribly frightened!"

The tears were running down her cheeks as Anona lifted her mother's best evening-gown out of the wardrobe.

Then as she heard her father coming up the stairs she wiped them fiercely away.

She had to be brave. She had to help him.

Yet, when he left her she would be alone and she would not even have a name.

chapter four

LORD Selwyn enjoyed, as he had expected, his trip through the Mediterranean and the Suez Canal.

This had been opened the previous month.

He was extremely interested in seeing the remarkable results of de Lesseps's engineering genius and administrative enterprise.

It had shortened the voyage to India to between seventeen and twenty days.

He had taken with him a number of books to read on the voyage.

Unfortunately he had nothing in his Library about Penang.

He wondered exactly what it would be like when he arrived there.

He tried not to think about Maisie.

Yet, when he went out on deck at night to look at the stars, he found himself thinking that the love he was seeking was something he would never find.

Were all women so treacherous?

Were all women liars?

Perhaps he had been unfortunate with the women he knew, and especially in the case of Maisie.

Because she was so young, and because he had believed her to be pure, she had awoken in him the chivalry he had known as a boy.

She had received his ideals about women, and then had disillusioned him.

"I was asking too much!" he told himself severely.

At the same time, he could not help wondering if every man became as disillusioned as he was.

He thought of the artists like Botticelli, who had painted the beauty of love so brilliantly.

He remembered the Composers like Chopin who when their music was played could arouse love.

There were the Poets who had made love for those who read their works seem so utterly desirable.

Could it all be just an illusion?

Was it a dream from which a man awoke to find himself in a barren desert lured there by a mirage?

Lord Selwyn was glad when the ship reached Calcutta and he could escape from his thoughts and feelings.

He had sent a cable to the Viceroy, who had taken office only that year.

It was an appointment Lord Selwyn had approved wholeheartedly.

The sixth Earl of Mayo was comparatively unknown in England.

But the choice of the Prime Minister, Mr. Disraeli, was a stroke of genius.

Lord Selwyn had met the Earl first some years ago when he had visited Ireland to buy horses for his father's Stud.

The Earl was a great sportsman and a spectacularly successful Master of the Kildare Hunt.

He had taken a fancy to Lord Selwyn and invited him to stay and hunt that Autumn.

By the time he left, Lord Selwyn, who was then Paul Wyn, and the Earl of Mayo had become close friends.

He drove from the ship in a Viceregal carriage with an escort of cavalry to Government House.

As he did so, Lord Selwyn felt excited at the idea of seeing his friend again in a new environment.

He was quite certain the Earl would make a success of what was one of the greatest positions in the world.

The Viceroy was waiting for him and held out his hands in delight when Lord Selwyn appeared.

He was a splendid figure of a man, tall, broad-shouldered, and powerfully built.

As Lord Selwyn remembered, he had in his face both determination and humour.

He had not changed during the years. Lord Selwyn was vividly conscious that his enthusiasm, his cheerful gaiety and personality, his magnetism which few could resist, was all still there.

"This is a surprise, Paul!" the Viceroy exclaimed. "I had no idea you were coming to India."

"I did not know myself until I learned that my great-uncle had left me a house and a Plantation in Penang," Lord Selwyn replied.

"Penang!" the Earl said. "It is a place I know nothing about, but it is delightful to have you out here in the East."

They sat down to talk about Ireland and horses.

It was not until later that evening that the subject of Penang came again into the conversation.

It was then one of the Viceroy's Council, the Law Member FitzJames Stephen said:

"I am extremely interested, My Lord, that you should be going to Penang. It is a lovely place, and I only wish I could accompany you."

"You have been there?" Lord Selwyn asked. "Then you can tell me something about it, for I really know nothing except that it is quite a small island."

Mr. FitzJames Stephen laughed.

"That is certainly true! Actually the first British settlement was established there in 1786."

Lord Selwyn raised his eye-brows.

He was surprised, if that was the case, that Penang did not feature more prominently in the English History Books.

"You will see in Penang," Mr. FitzJames Stephen went on, "the British Raj in miniature. There is Fort Cornwallis called after our famous General, while George Town comprises an almost perfect mixture of English, Malayan, and Chinese."

Lord Selwyn was listening intently, and he went on:

"There is, of course, a Cricket Club, a Race-Course, and a very impressive Church, in fact, everything an Englishman requires abroad."

Both men laughed as FitzJames Stephen continued:

"As you are going there knowing nothing, I will cable to a friend of mine who is the principal Chinese on the island."

"Chinese?" Lord Selwyn asked.

He had expected to be put in touch with an Englishman.

As if he knew what he was thinking, Mr. FitzJames Stephen said:

"Lin Kuan Teng will, I am sure, make you more comfortable and even more welcome than the English could."

He paused and then continued:

"He is one of the most interesting men I have ever met, and he also happens to own the largest and most impressive house in George Town. It has been called a miniature Buckingham Palace, but is about the same size."

Lord Selwyn laughed.

"Well, I accept your suggestion with pleasure!"

"Lin Kuan Teng will look after you," Mr. Stephen said, "and anything you want will be procured with a flick of his long-nailed fingers!"

Lord Selwyn asked a great many questions of FitzJames Stephen in the next few days.

He learned about Captain Francis Light, an Englishman who had first seen the possibilities of Penang.

He was, in fact, the real Founder of the island.

There were only fifty-eight men, women, and children living on Penang when he first went there.

He believed that its natural habour and the geographical position of the island could be of tremendous importance to the British.

"He is one of the great heroes of our Empire," FitzJames Stephen said, "and, of course, like most of us, appreciated only when he was dead."

"I am afraid that is true," Lord Selwyn agreed.

When he was alone with the Viceroy, the Earl said to him:

"What are you doing with your life, Paul?"

He paused and then continued:

"You know you are much cleverer than the average Englishman of your age, and you should not be wasting your time with a lot of bird-witted women."

"What do you mean by that?" Lord Selwyn asked.

"I hear about you from time to time," the Viceroy replied, "and it is invariably because your name has been associated with some woman whose claim to fame is that she has a beautiful face."

Lord Selwyn did not answer, and the Viceroy went on:

"I know you have been brilliantly successful in some of the Diplomatic missions on which you have embarked, but frankly, Paul, I believe you to be capable of greater things."

Lord Selwyn held up his hands in protest.

"There is always somebody trying to make me do something different!" he complained. "My family want me to marry, and you want me to work harder!"

"I want you to make the most of your talents and not waste them as you have been doing," the Viceroy replied.

He spoke seriously.

Then with one of his irresistible smiles he added:

"When I first met you, Paul, I knew you were not only one of the cleverest young men I had ever met, but you had a remarkable personality. That is a hard thing to find these days."

"Are you suggesting that I should follow in your footsteps and become a Viceroy?" Lord Selwyn asked.

He was speaking mockingly, but the Viceroy said quite seriously:

"It is certainly a possibility, and I can imagine it as an Office in which you would be extremely successful."

"Now you are really frightening me!" Lord Selwyn exclaimed.

There was a short silence, then he added:

"At the same time, I would rather follow your advice than be married to some woman with whom I became utterly bored and inevitably disillusioned within two weeks of our wedding!"

He spoke bitterly, and the Viceroy said, using his Irish perception:

"I think you have been hurt. It is something that happens to all of us at one time or another."

"Not exactly hurt," Lord Selwyn replied, "but it is always upsetting to find one is a fool, if only to one's self."

The Viceroy smiled.

"That, too, is something that happens to us all sooner or later."

He paused and then went on:

"But believe me, Paul, when I tell you quite frankly that I know you are capable of great things, and that is what must really matter in your life."

"It sounds very flattering," Lord Selwyn said. "At the same time, I have no idea how to begin to live up to your estimation of me."

The Viceroy made an expressive gesture with his hands.

"It is something which will come to you," he said, "I am quite certain of that. As you know, Paul, I have used my perception all my life and it has never failed me.''

He paused, then went on:

"I suppose it is my Irish blood that makes it possible for me to know exactly what a man is like the moment I meet him.''

He smiled before he went on:

"It is an ability that has always served me in good stead.''

"Did you ever think you would be offered this particular post?'' Lord Selwyn asked curiously.

"Not exactly this; in fact, I never aspired so high,'' the Earl replied. "But I think I was always aware that Fate had other things for me besides being the Master of the Kildare Hunt!''

His voice deepened as he said:

"It was the terrible years of famine in Ireland which prepared me for the spectre of famine that I find here. It was the years as Irish Chief Secretary that taught me how to govern.''

"Of one thing I am completely certain,'' Lord Selwyn said, "and I do not need to use any special perception, and that is that you will be an outstanding and entirely successful Viceroy.''

"Thank you!'' the Earl said. "That is what I hope to be, but at the moment, Paul, I am thinking of you and not of myself!''

* * *

It was with the Viceroy's words still ringing in his ears that Lord Selwyn left Calcutta the following week for Penang.

Everything had been arranged for him by Mr. Fitz-James Stephen.

He was seen off with a great deal of pomp and Vice-regal splendour.

This ensured that he was received in the same way aboard the ship.

He was therefore not surprised when they docked in the harbour of George Town to find a large deputation waiting to receive him.

There was a number of British who were obviously overawed that he should have come straight from the Viceroy.

But it was Lin Kuan Teng who greeted him with the most respectful bows and the inevitable flowery language.

He had, Lord Selwyn realised at once, the foreceful personality of which FitzJames Stephen had spoken.

It was Lin Kuan Teng's carriage in which he drove away from the quayside.

His house, he informed Lord Selwyn, was just outside the main part of George Town.

It was very large and of white stone, a heavily porticoed entrance and Grecian pillars supporting an open balcony.

It was, he thought with a smile, even more impressive than Buckingham Palace.

Inside, the Chinese pictures, the jade, and pink quartz as well as the porcelain were overwhelming.

There was a collection of Tang horses that Lord Selwyn thought he would give his whole fortune to possess.

The rugs on the floor were so priceless that they should have been hung rather than walked upon.

Lin Kuan Teng had a charming wife and three beautiful daughters.

His son, he explained, was at the docks overseeing his ships, of which he owned a considerable number.

The ship carrying Lord Selwyn had arrived in the morning.

By the time he reached Lin Kuan Teng's house it was time for luncheon.

He knew, when he tasted the delicious Chinese food, that FitzJames Stephen had not exaggerated when he said he would be comfortable.

"I had a most respectful admiration for your honourable great-uncle, My Lord," his Chinese host said. "It was a great joy to have such a distinguished man on the island, and to seek his advice on matters of Law."

"It was a great surprise to me," Lord Selwyn replied, "that he left me his house and Plantation."

"One of the very best on Penang," Lin Kuan Teng replied. "His Lordship grew spices, and his crops brought him in a considerable amount of money. I think you will also appreciate the contents of his house."

"If, even in a small way, they compare with the treasures you have here," Lord Selwyn said, "I shall consider myself very, very lucky!"

Lin Kuan Teng bowed at the compliment, then said:

"Your honourable great-uncle brought many things with him from Hong Kong. He was also an ardent buyer in the Bazaars in George Town, where the Chinese display their goods."

"I shall look forward to seeing them for myself," Lord Selwyn replied.

"I will take care that you are not deceived or robbed," his host promised.

As luncheon finished, Lord Selwyn suggested that he should visit his new property.

"That is what I expected you would want to do as soon as possible," Lin Kuan Teng replied, "but may I humbly suggest it is the wrong time of day."

He paused a moment then went on:

"It is getting very, very hot, and it is always a mistake to move quickly or hurry as soon as you arrive."

He smiled as he said:

"Take the advice of an older man, My Lord, and rest for this afternoon. Tomorrow, early in the morning, one of my carriages will take you to your house."

He stopped before continuing:

"You will see it and its beautiful surroundings looking their best."

Lord Selwyn knew he was talking good sense.

He was indeed finding it very hot despite the fact that there were *punkah*s moving slowly backwards and forwards overhead.

All the doors and windows in the house were wide open, but there was no breeze.

He therefore allowed himself to be shown to the bedroom, where he would sleep until he could make other arrangements.

He found it was a large, impressive room with windows looking out to sea.

There was a garden directly in front, and the green grass obviously was watered frequently.

It led through bushes heavy with blossom down to a sandy bay which was enclosed on either side by trees.

Trees also encircled the house so that it could not be seen from the roadway.

Lord Selwyn thought his host had certainly chosen the most beautiful spot anyone could imagine.

He was rather sorry that his great-uncle had settled inland rather than near the sea.

However, he was not prepared to criticise until he had seen his property to-morrow.

Higgins helped him to undress and almost immediately after he lay down he fell asleep.

*   *   *

When Lord Selwyn awoke the sun had lost much of its strength, but it was still hot.

He could hear the sound of the *punkah* moving over his head.

Without calling a servant he dressed himself in a white shirt and white trousers. Then he walked out through the open window into the garden.

The flowers were fantastic and brilliant with colour.

He had never seen so many butterflies.

He was also aware that there were birds singing in the trees and thought their names were another thing he must learn.

He also wanted to know what other creatures were indigenous to the island.

"A new country, new friends, and, perhaps—a new life!"

He toyed with the idea of coming to live in Penang and forgetting about England.

Then he remembered what the Viceroy had said to him.

Suddenly he felt annoyed at the idea of being pushed into being more important than he was already.

"Why should I trouble?" he asked himself. "Why should I worry about anything except enjoying myself?"

Then he added:

"I wish people would leave me alone. I want to live my own life and not be manipulated by anybody, however well-meaning their intentions may be."

He walked back into the house.

There being no sign of his host, he started to inspect the amazing treasures that Lin Kuan Teng had collected.

Lord Selwyn was very knowledgeable about English and Continental pictures and furniture.

But he realised he had a great deal to learn about Chinese art.

The examples he could see were exquisite and, he knew, very old.

He thought it would take a lifetime to understand them.

He said much the same thing to his host when he reappeared, having also, Lord Selwyn was sure, slept peacefully.

"The Chinese appreciate antiquity perhaps more than anybody else because they worship it," Lin Kuan Teng replied.

"I suppose that is true," Lord Selwyn said, "but it is extraordinary that a country which to the modern world seems backward could ever have produced such amazing Works of Art!"

"I think you find them interesting," Lin Kuan Teng said, "because they are all drawn, painted, or carved to convey a spiritual message."

"Exactly!" Lin Kuan Teng agreed. "And to us they

are not merely beautiful, but have a teaching which we appreciate with our spirit as well as with our eyes.''

Lord Selwyn knew this was true.

Even so, when Lin Kuan Teng showed him some intricate carvings, it seemed impossible they had been done by an ordinary man.

Every picture had a hidden significance which stimulated the mind.

Because he knew it was difficult for a Western man to comprehend this, he wanted to know more.

In fact, he sat talking to Lin Kuan Teng until it was very late. His host's wife and daughters had long retired to bed.

When he was alone, he undressed and lay in the comfortable bed made up on a low divan.

It was then he knew that his conversation with Lin Kuan Teng had made him aware of new horizons.

He told himself as he closed his eyes that so far Penang fascinated him.

* * *

Lord Selwyn was awoken early when the sun had not yet risen.

Only its first pale gold rays were sweeping away the darkness and the stars.

The air coming through the open windows was fresh.

As Lord Selwyn dressed, he thought with excitement of what he was going to see to-day.

Lin Kuan Teng had arranged for the Solicitors of his great-uncle's estate to follow them in another carriage.

''You travel with me,'' his host said firmly. ''Too much chatter disturbs the mind and you miss the new views, new beauty. Look in silence. Much better.''

"I agree with you,'' Lord Selwyn answered.

When he was dressed he looked out of one of the windows.

He saw his host walking across the green lawn towards the sea.

Because there was a great deal more he wanted to ask him, he hurried after him.

When he caught him up, Lin Kuan Teng bowed and said:

"I hope, my most honourable guest, that you were comfortable last night in my humble home.''

Because he knew this was the correct form of address, Lord Selwyn prevented himself from laughing.

For his host's Palace to be described as ''humble'' was ridiculous.

"I slept peacefully,'' he replied, ''and I thank you most gratefully for your kind and gracious hospitality.''

Lin Kuan Teng bowed again, and they walked on towards the sea.

The way was beautiful.

Birds, bluebirds, and the black and white Magpie Robins were singing in the trees.

Butterflies fluttered over the flowers and shrubs.

Occasionally a small lizard hurried away before their feet.

It was only a short distance to the bay.

As it opened up in front of them, Lord Selwyn thought it impossible for sand to be more golden.

The sea itself was the green of the jade Buddhas in Lin Kuan Teng's collection.

Then, as he could see the bay and the sea merging

into a misty horizon, he heard Lin Kuan Teng give an exclamation.

He turned towards his host in surprise.

He was looking to where in the near curve of the bay there was a boat.

It seemed to Lord Selwyn quite an ordinary boat.

It was stranded half on the sand and half in the water.

Lin Kuan Teng walked quickly towards it, so he followed him.

As he drew nearer he saw what he had not noticed at first: there was somebody in the boat.

The Chinese did not speak.

His face was impassive, but Lord Selwyn was aware that he was annoyed that the boat should be there.

He could understand that the bay, being private, its owner would certainly resent intruders.

If there was one, he must be hiding, determined not to draw attention to himself.

It took the two men only a few minutes to walk across the sands and reach the boat.

Then, as Lin Kuan Teng stood looking down at what it contained, Lord Selwyn joined him.

Lying in the bottom of the boat, her head on a silk pillow, was the most beautiful girl he had ever seen.

She was so beautiful and so elaborately dressed that Lord Selwyn felt he must be dreaming.

He shut his eyes, thinking he had been dazzled by the sun.

But as he opened them again she was still there.

Her long eye-lashes were dark against her very pale cheeks.

Her hair was golden on the silk pillow and her skin was translucent like a pearl.

She was wearing, Lord Selwyn noted with surprise, what appeared to be a very elaborate evening-gown.

Round her neck was a diamond necklace.

There were also diamonds on her wrists and on her bodice.

She was spread out in the boat from which, and this was strange, the oarsmen's benches had been removed.

Her pillow was of white satin, and she was lying on what appeared to be several satin-covered cushions.

At last Lord Selwyn found his voice:

"Who is she? How did she come to be here?"

As he asked the question he would not have been surprised if Lin Kuan Teng replied that she was from another Planet.

Never had he imagined that any woman could be so beautiful, with a beauty that was ethereal and hardly human.

It seemed a long time before Lin Kuan Teng spoke.

Then he said:

"I have no idea who the lady could be or where she has come from. Very strange. Very mysterious! Perhaps she may be a gift from the gods!"

*　　*　　*

Anona had been more and more frightened as, having boarded her father's ship, they set off at a tremendous speed out to sea.

She was terrified that at any moment they would find a Naval ship following them.

Then her father would be arrested.

As soon as she was ready, he had taken her from the house down to the beach.

He was carrying the small case in which she had placed her mother's gown and jewels.

It also contained her own things for the night.

While she was packing, Anona had heard her father talking to Chang.

He was giving him instructions to look after the house in their absence.

She guessed her father had also given Chang a large sum of money.

"If I am not back for some time, you look after everything, Chang, and do not let anybody steal from the house."

"No, no, Master," Chang answered. "Keep watch. No thieves! No robbers!"

He was smiling delightedly so that Anona knew he now had plenty of money for his wife and family.

On the beach there was the rowing-boat.

Her father had helped her into it and as he rowed away from the shore she wondered where they were going.

How could they travel far in only a rowing-boat.

Her father had turned North, and, rowing very fast, they went past the houses on stilts.

The women and children waved to them, and Anona waved back.

She knew they would think it odd if she did not do so.

At the same time, she wanted to cry. She was leaving her home, everything that was familiar, and, most of all, the memories of her mother.

How could this have happened?

How could she face the future alone?

About half-a-mile up the coast there was a bay in which there were no houses.

The trees that lined the shore were so thick that it had become a jungle.

It was here Anona had seen her father's ship, and waiting on its deck were his two friends.

They were, she knew, watching eagerly for his return so that they could get away as quickly as possible.

She was helped aboard by her father, and he introduced her to the two Englishmen.

One was about the same age as herself, the other younger.

Immediately the engines had started up and they steered out to sea.

Soon they were moving faster than Anona had thought any ship could travel.

It was only as darkness came that they slowed their pace.

She noticed then that they had no port or starboard lights on the ship.

She had learned there were four Chinese as crew, and no one else.

There were three comfortable cabins below, and after a light meal she went to her father's.

He told her to get undressed and get into bed.

When she had done so he came to say good-night.

He sat down on the mattress facing her and, taking her hand in his, said quickly:

"You are very brave, my darling, and I am very proud of you."

"I . . . I am frightened . . . Papa . . . very frightened!"

Anona answered. "But the only . . . thing that really matters is . . . when . . . shall I . . . see you . . . again?"

"I told you, my precious, that I will communicate with you as soon as it is safe for me to do so. But I plan to go a long way from here."

"Where . . . to?" Anona asked.

"First to Taiwan, then possibly to China."

"Oh, Papa, will it be . . . safe?"

"I hope so," her father answered, "but I cannot plan the future. I can only live from day to day."

"I shall pray, Papa . . . I shall pray . . . every day . . . and . . . every moment!" Anona said passionately.

"That is what I want you do do," her father said. "And as you have already told me, my darling, that your mother will be looking after me, I know she will look after you."

Anona's fingers tightened on his as she pleaded:

"Please . . . Papa . . . take me with you . . . I would not mind . . . anything . . . however difficult it is . . . as long as I could be . . . with you."

She saw the pain in her father's eyes.

"It is something I want more than Heaven itself," he replied. "But if I took you, it would be just being selfish."

He paused a moment and then went on:

"I have to think of your future, and the one thing is for you to be with people who are respectable and not criminals like me!"

Anona gave a little cry.

"You are not to speak like that, Papa! Of course you are not a criminal! To me you are good, kind, and wonderful, very, very wonderful . . . and that is how I shall always remember you.''

Her father bent forward to kiss her, and she thought there were tears in his eyes.

Then, as if he could not bear any more, he said:

''Go to sleep, my precious, I will wake you when it is time to leave.''

He walked from the cabin and Anona cried herself to sleep.

*　　*　　*

Anona felt as if she had not been asleep for very long when her father called her.

''It is time, my precious,'' he said.

She got out of bed and he helped her to dress in her mother's evening-gown and jewellery.

He pinned the large diamond star which he had given her mother for Christmas to the front of her bodice.

''A star to guide me!'' he said beneath his breath.

Anona was too miserable to speak.

He led her gently from the cabin and up the companionway.

She wanted to ask him questions; there were a thousand things she wanted to say to him.

But she seemed to have lost her voice.

Her father's friends were waiting, and as they joined them, she heard her father ask:

''Is everything ready?''

''Exactly as you wanted it.''

He turned to Anona.

''We have some coffee ready for you,'' he said. ''I

want you to drink it, as you must not feel thirsty before you are found.''

Anona clenched her fingers together.

She wanted to scream that she could not leave him, could not face the future alone.

But they were waiting, and she thought it would be humiliating if she made a scene in front of his friends.

One of them held out a cup to her, and she took it from him, her eyes on her father's face.

She was thinking how handsome he looked and how much she loved him.

Because she loved him, she knew she must do as he asked her even though the agony was almost tearing her apart.

Without even realising what she was doing, she drank the cup of coffee.

Only as she handed back the cup did she feel her head begin to swim and the deck seemed to slip away beneath her.

She tried to cry out, but it was too late.

There was only darkness, and she knew no more.

chapter five

ANONA came back to consciousness and opened her eyes.

It was only as she saw a strange room that she remembered what had happened.

She shut her eyes again quickly, trying to make her brain work.

She felt as if it were stuffed with cotton-wool.

All she could recall was her father's face and how much she loved him.

Then she remembered her fear at what she had to do, and was aware of what had happened.

She realised now that he had drugged her coffee.

She knew that when she had lost consciousness he must have carried her into the boat.

She had asked him how he was to make sure that the boat landed on the shore of his friend's private beach.

Her father had smiled.

"You may be quite certain, my darling, I will not let you be carried away by the tide."

"H-how can you be . . . sure?" Anona had asked.

She was afraid that because she was wearing her mother's jewellery, she might be robbed, or perhaps killed by Pirates.

In any case, they would think an empty boat was something for them to acquire.

"I am a good swimmer," her father replied.

"You mean," Anona asked, "you will . . . come with . . . me?"

"I shall swim beside the boat and guide it," her father replied, "so I promise you, my precious little daughter, that you will land exactly where I want you to."

That had been reassuring.

Yet now that she had arrived at her destination she was even more frightened.

She was alone, completely alone in a strange house on a strange island.

Her whole being shrank from the interrogation that lay ahead of her.

She longed to escape into the darkness and remain unconscious—perhaps for ever.

With her eyes still shut she was aware, although the movement was very soft, there was somebody in the room.

Whoever it was was near her, looking at her, then moved away.

Finally, because she wanted more than anything else something to drink, she opened her eyes again.

Now she saw the same white ceiling she had seen before.

As she stared at it, afraid to look lower, a voice asked:

"You 'wake, Lady?"

It spoke in pidgin English, and Anona thought with relief that this was something which she was used to.

Slowly she lowered her eyes to see the face of a Chinese woman.

She might easily have been one of the Chinese she had known and talked to when she was at home.

"W-where . . . am . . . I?" Anona asked.

It was difficult to say the words because her mouth was so dry.

She knew it was because of the drug she had been given in the coffee.

She thought she had been very foolish to have drunk it without guessing why her father was giving it to her.

At the same time, everything must have gone according to plan.

She could see that the room in which she was lying was luxurious, the furniture valuable.

The sheet that covered her was of silk.

Someone must have undressed her, because she was no longer wearing her mother's evening-gown.

The diamond necklace had been removed, and also the bracelets.

As if she knew what she wanted, the Chinese maid asked:

"Drink, Missy. Feel better."

She held a glass to Anona's lips and with a skilled hand raised her head a little.

Anona drank thirstily, thinking the fruit juice was delicious.

It certainly took away the dryness in her mouth.

She hoped that soon her brain would feel clearer and not so muzzy.

"Lady safe," the Chinese maid said. "Go sleep. Very hot."

What she said told Anona that it must be after midday and the sun was too fierce for people to move about.

She suspected the Chinese to whom her father had sent her would also be resting, and his family too.

'I suppose I shall have to meet them sooner or later,' she thought.

She felt herself tremble.

The maid left her and she slipped away into the darkness to dream of her father.

*   *   *

When Anona awoke again the maid was raising the sub-blinds over the windows.

Anona knew it must be late in the afternoon.

She moved her head to look round at the room, and the maid came to the bed-side to say:

"You better?"

"I . . . I think . . . so," Anona replied tentatively.

"Master wish meet you."

For a moment Anona could not reply.

Then she told herself she could not go on sleeping for ever.

It would be best to get the ordeal over rather than have it hanging over her head.

Very slowly, because she feared it might hurt her, she sat up in bed.

To her relief, she no longer felt as if it was impossible to think and her brain would not work.

She had a slight headache and once again she was thirsty.

"Please . . . may I have . . . a drink?" she asked.

"Have ready."

The maid brought a small tray and put it on the bed beside her.

On it was a glass filled with fruit juice and two plates.

On one there were fruits of all kinds, which were familiar to Anona.

On the other there were small sweetmeats made from honey and nuts which she had often had before.

She drank the fruit juice.

And because she thought it was a sensible thing to do, she ate one of the sweetmeats and a little of the fruit.

The maid waited on the other side of the room until she had finished.

As she removed the tray she said:

"Lady rise, I help."

She put the tray down on the table and came back to the bed to help Anona step onto the floor.

As her bare feet touched the soft velvet of the exquisite patterned rug, she found she was not giddy.

She was, in fact, she knew, almost free of the drug that had rendered her unconscious.

After she had washed, there was nothing for her to put on except the evening-gown in which she had arrived.

As the maid buttoned it down the back, she thought it over-elaborate.

Surely her host would think it looked very strange.

Then she remembered what her father had said.

The gown was a clue to her identity which they must never know.

It would ensure that she was treated with respect.

As the maid clasped the bracelet round her wrist, Anona thought:

'At least they will not turn me out of the house into the street dressed like this!'

It was cold comfort, but better than nothing.

The maid tidied her hair, and Anona looked at herself in the mirror.

It had a beautifully carved gold frame.

She somehow expected she would look quite different after all that had occurred.

Strangely enough, she found she looked very much as usual.

Except that it seemed unusual to be wearing her mother's glittering diamond necklace.

She was pale, but that, she thought, was what anyone would expect her to be.

She stared at herself for quite some minutes, trying to think what she would say.

She was reminding herself of how careful she must be not to reveal anything.

She knew it could be dangerous for her father if she made any mistakes.

"Help me, Mama, help me," she prayed.

She turned from the mirror to where the Chinese woman was waiting for her at the door.

"Lady ready?" she asked. "I take you to Master."

Just for a moment a sudden panic made Anona want to reply that she was too ill and must go back to bed.

Then she told herself she would not be afraid.

Her father had been brave enough to behave in a reprehensible and dangerous way because he loved her mother and her.

She would not fail him now by playing the coward.

Walking carefully in the satin slippers which went with her gown, she moved slowly across the room.

The Chinese woman opened the door.

Then as they both went outside she went ahead.

She led the way through cool corridors until they came to what Anona guessed was the centre of the house.

Now she drew in a deep breath as the maid went through an open door and she followed.

She found herself in a magnificent room which she saw at a glance was filled with treasures which her father would have appreciated.

There were pictures, inlaid and gilt furniture, and two cabinets that she was sure contained the jade and porcelain that both she and her mother had loved.

At the same time, she was acutely aware of someone who was there.

At the end of the room, seated on a chair which seemed to her like a throne, was a Chinese.

In his Mandarin's robes he was even more impressive and overwhelming than she had expected.

Slowly she walked towards him.

Ahead of her the Chinese woman went down on her knees and touched the floor with her forehead.

In Chinese she said:

"The Lady has awakened, Most Honourable Master, after long sleep."

Lin Kuan Teng's eyes were on Anona.

As she reached him she dropped him a low curtsy and he rose to his feet.

"I am honoured, Madam, that you should visit me," he said in good English, "but mystified as to why you should do so."

The Chinese woman withdrew.

Anona, speaking very slowly, said:

"Not as . . . mystified as . . . I am, Honoured Sir."

Lin Kuan Teng smiled.

"I think we should sit down," he suggested, "and you must tell me exactly what happened."

As he spoke he indicated a comfortable sofa that was near the open window.

Anona moved towards it thankfully.

She felt she needed air and she was also afraid of standing.

She knew it was not weakness but fear.

At the same time, she kept thinking of her father and trying to remember what he had instructed her to say.

The sofa was comfortable and Western.

She noticed there were a great number of stools and cushions in the room.

There was an armchair with a high back near the sofa, and Lin Kuan Teng seated himself in it.

He looked, Anona thought, so like some of the ancient pictures she had seen of Chinese Mandarins, it was difficult to believe he was real.

As if he were aware that she was nervous, he said:

"Now, tell me what happened to you."

Anona made a helpless little gesture with her hands.

"I have been . . . thinking about that . . . ever since I . . . woke up . . . and . . . I do not know."

"What do you mean—you do not know?"

"I . . . cannot remember!"

Lin Kuan Teng looked at her as if he did not believe what he had heard.

Then he said:

"Let us, Gracious Lady, start at the beginning. What is your name?"

Anona was silent. Then after a long pause she said:

"I . . . I am . . . trying very h-hard . . . but I cannot . . . remember."

"Can you recall from where you came?"

Anona shook her head.

Because she was afraid she was stretching his credibility too far, she said hesitatingly:

"My . . . head it . . . tender . . . I think . . . perhaps I was struck on the head."

"You have no idea who or what it could have been?"

"N-no."

"Or where you were when it happened?"

"No."

Lin Kuan Teng's enigmatic face showed no emotion.

Anona was aware that he was not only surprised but nonplussed.

He put the long-nailed fingers of his hands together as he said:

"We can assume that you were aboard a ship, because I found you in my bay in a small boat."

Anona opened her eyes wider.

"I . . . I came in a . . . boat?"

"You do not know that?"

She shook her head.

"Then let me explain," Lin Kuan Teng said. "I found you in the bay which is at the bottom of my garden."

He paused and then continued:

"You were lying in a boat on satin cushions, dressed as you are now."

Anona made a little murmur and looked down at the skirt of her gown.

It had frills of lace in which were caught small bunches of musk roses.

She had thought when her mother wore it that it was the most beautiful gown she had ever seen.

She felt sure the Chinese opposite her, with his shrewd eyes, would appreciate that it had been very expensive.

It was in a fashion that had just come from Paris.

At the back there was a bustle which her mother told her had been the creation of Frederick Worth.

He was the English Dress Designer who had signed the death warrant of the crinoline.

She could remember her mother saying that when she appeared in the gown at the Governor's Ball, the women who were not so up-to-date looked as if they could scratch her eyes out.

"But your father was very proud of me," she had added softly, "and that was the only thing that mattered."

Now, as Lin Kuan Teng wanted to question her, Anona felt that both her father and mother were helping her to give the right answers.

Lin Kuan Teng tried to help her recall from where she had come and to where she had been going.

He asked her about her family, who her father was, if she could remember either him or her mother.

At first she either shook her head, or said "No."

As the interrogation continued, however, she just sat, looking helpless.

Finally Lin Kuan Teng admitted defeat.

"I am sure," he said kindly, "the gods will give you back your memory sooner or later. It is just a question of waiting."

"But . . . where shall . . . I wait?" Anona asked.

She knew as she spoke that this was the important question.

"There is plenty of room for you here," he answered, "and you will honour my house with your beauty."

Anona smiled for the first time since she had come into the room.

"Thank you . . . thank you!" she cried. "I have been so . . . afraid while we have been . . . talking that you would . . . send me . . . away."

"I am not a cruel man," Lin Kuan Teng said. "I am sure it will not be long before you remember who you are. Then I will find your family and friends."

"You are . . . very kind."

Lin Kuan Teng rose from his chair.

"And now," he said, "you must meet my family. As you can imagine, they are very curious about you, and think perhaps you have dropped down from Heaven, or come from the depths of the sea."

Anona laughed.

"Perhaps that is true, but if it was from the sea, I would be a mermaid and have a tail!"

He escorted her to another part of the house to meet his family.

She thought, as they walked, that everything had gone better than she had expected.

She could almost hear her father laugh and say:

"Good girl! You have done exactly as I told you to do!"

*   *   *

Lord Selwyn had enjoyed seeing his new possessions even more than he had expected.

He had, in fact, been astonished by the house and delighted by its position.

He had expected, because his great-uncle had been such a clever man, that anything he built would be at least pleasant and moderately comfortable.

What he had not anticipated, however, was that Lord Durham would have erected a replica of an English house designed in the middle of the last century.

Lord Selwyn was in Penang, yet he might have been looking at the home of one of his aristocratic friends in England.

There was the same perfectly proportioned architecture, the same Ionic pillars at the top of a row of steps.

There were long, Georgian windows looking over the Plantation below.

Lord Selwyn knew that Lin Kuan Teng was watching his reaction, and as they drove up to the front-door, he exclaimed:

"I do not believe it! I expected the house to be slightly European, but not an excellent imitation of the work of the brothers Adam!"

He was not surprised that Lin Kuan Teng was aware that the two Adam brothers were the greatest Architects of the eighteenth century.

"I knew you would be surprised, My Lord!" he replied in an amused voice. "But this was your honourable great-uncle's home, and he wanted it to be as English as possible."

"If he felt so strongly," Lord Selwyn replied, "I cannot imagine why he did not return to live in England."

"He once said to me that, as he had been in the East for so long, he thought like a Chinese, ate like one, and was more at home with the Chinese than with his own people.''

Lord Selwyn smiled, but he did not interrupt as Lin Kuan Teng went on:

''But I think your Honourable Relative dreamt of England, and that was why when he could build a house of his dreams he built this.''

If the outside was not what Lord Selwyn had expected, the inside, to his delight, was filled with the treasures he had hoped to find there.

They were, of course, not the equal of those he had admired in Lin Kuan Teng's Palace.

Yet there was some porcelain he knew he was unique in owning.

There was also jade, pink quartz, and crystal, as well as pictures which decorated the walls.

Lin Kuan Teng could tell him who were the artists and the dates when they had been painted.

He also knew the history of most of the pieces of furniture.

''Your honourable great-uncle asked me to help him in their selection, and we instructed the Chinese to bring what we required, and they seldom disappointed us.''

Lord Selwyn would have been very churlish if he had not realised how fortunate he was.

How could he have expected to be left possessions so unusual and so priceless?

When he had inspected Durham House, as it was called, Lin Kuan Teng left him.

''I send the carriage back for you, My Lord,'' he said.''

Lord Selwyn was now in the hands of the Solicitors,

who were eager to show him the Plantation.

It was quite large, but Lord Selwyn said he wished to see the gardens.

They had grown slightly wild, but were very beautiful.

As Lord Selwyn expected, there was a profusion of orchids, including the pure white creamy-petalled Phalaenopis.

He was also delighted that he had a tree which he had learnt the Malayans called *Serac*.

The flowers bloomed straight out of the bark.

There were so many things he wanted to inspect in the garden alone.

But he realised that what they wanted to show him were the crops on the Plantation.

They assured him the land, if tended, would bring him a considerable income every year.

Of course he was interested.

But it was the unusual beauty of the treasures in the house and the flowers in the garden which he knew he would remember when he returned to England.

"If you are interested in orchids, Honourable Lord," the Chinese Solicitor said, "you will certainly need to stay in Penang for a long time."

He spoke hopefully, and Lord Selwyn enquired:

"Why do you say that?"

The Chinese smiled.

"We have eight-hundred species of orchid in Malaya," he replied. "There is one of them!"

He pointed to an exquisite blossom hanging from the trunk of a lichened tree.

Lord Selwyn laughed.

"I can see I shall have to get busy right away, otherwise I shall find myself spending my life here, like my great-uncle.''

He spoke jokingly. He was astonished to realise from the expression on the faces of the men who were listening that that was exactly what they hoped he would do.

'They will be disappointed!' he thought.

But he knew it would be a mistake to tell them so.

He was well aware how he would get the best information from them.

It would be by letting them think he intended to work the Plantation and live in the house, as his great-uncle had done.

There was, he thought, fortunately, no reason, or even possibility, for him to move in immediately.

There were no servants and only two old Caretakers.

He could therefore continue to be comfortable with Lin Kuan Teng.

He, however, enjoyed a Chinese meal which the Solicitors had brought with them.

He listened to everything they told him and gave the Caretakers enough money to make them gasp with delight.

Then, late in the afternoon, when it was not so hot, he drove in an open carriage to George Town.

He would have been very unobservant if he had not realised how beautiful the journey was.

The trees, the wild flowers, the birds, which he realised were all new to him, were entrancing.

So were the small children, Malayan or Chinese, playing about beside the dusty road.

Older boys were climbing up the palm trees to shake down the coconuts.

When he arrived in George Town he was feeling elated with his new possession.

He was glad that he had somebody as intelligent as Lin Kuan Teng to talk to.

He was aware that, as FitzJames Stephen had said, he was a very exceptional man.

It amused Lord Selwyn to think that he had had to come as far as Penang to find him, a man whose conversation he enjoyed as much as he enjoyed being with Mr. Benjamin Disraeli, the Prime Minister.

'I suppose, in a way,' he ruminated to himself, 'they are both Oriental, and therefore quick-witted, more sensitive, and certainly more perceptive than the average Englishman.'

He drove through the gate and into the blossom-filled garden of Lin Kuan Teng's house.

As he did so, he was thinking eagerly of a dozen questions he wished to put to his host.

Only as he stepped from the carriage did he remember the strange young woman who had been washed up on the beach early in the morning.

He thought that by now they would have discovered who she was, in which case she would have already gone back to where she had come from.

He would have liked to look at her again, because she was undoubtedly unusually lovely.

She was almost, he thought, like one of the Chinese goddesses carved out of crystal in the cabinet of the big Sitting-Room.

Then he laughed at himself for being so interested in her.

After all, she was a woman, and at the moment women were very much his *bête noire*.

'I expect when she is consicous,' he thought, 'I will be disillusioned. She may even be cross-eyed!'

He was mocking at himself as he entered the house.

A servant escorted him directly to where Lin Kuan Teng was sitting with his wife and daughters.

They were on the large balcony with pillars which looked out onto the garden.

There was no glass between the pillars, and they could breathe what movement there was in the warm, moist air.

At the same time, the *punkah*s were moving overhead.

Lin Kuan Teng's wife and daughters were seated on low stools and cushions.

His host was seated on a high-backed Mandarin's throne.

He looked, Lord Selwyn thought, almost like a King.

As he walked towards him, Lord Selwyn saw that seated beside him, also on a high-backed chair, was the young woman he had seen that morning in the boat.

She was listening with rapt attention to something Lin Kuan Teng was saying to her.

Her eyes were raised, and her small, pointed face was framed like a halo by her hair.

It seemed to be as golden as the sunlight.

For a moment Lord Selwyn could only look at her, thinking, as he had that morning, that he was dreaming.

It was impossible that anyone could look so lovely and yet be real.

Then, as Lin Kuan Teng saw him, he rose to say:

"Welcome back, Most Honourable Guest, from your 'Voyage of Discovery'!"

It flashed through Lord Selwyn's mind that if *he* had discovered something rare, his host had something equally as precious beside him.

He replied in his usual dignified manner:

"I have a great deal to tell you, but for the moment I am delighted to be back in your beautiful house again and to be with you and your family."

As he spoke he could not help looking towards the obvious exception to what he had just said.

Lin Kuan Teng followed the direction of his eyes.

"May I present, My Lord," he said, "somebody else who honours my poor home with her presence?"

He indicated Anona as he spoke.

She rose from her chair and curtsied to Lord Selwyn, who held out his hand.

"I believe you are English," he said, "and it is delightful for me to meet someone from my own country."

He felt Anona's fingers flutter in his and knew she was frightened.

He did not know why, but instinctively he felt he wanted to help her.

"My name is Selwyn," he added, as Lin Kuan Teng had not mentioned it.

There was a pause as he waited for her to reply.

Then, while he still held her hand, Anona said in a low voice:

"I . . . I have . . . forgotten what . . . my name is!"

She spoke as if the words were almost dragged from her.

Lord Selwyn raised his eye-brows in surprise, and Lin Kuan Teng explained:

"This beautiful Lady, whom you and I found in a boat on my beach, My Lord, has lost her memory!"

"Lost her memory?" Lord Selwyn repeated in astonishment.

Then, as he looked into the eyes of the lovely creature facing him, he saw she was frightened—very, very frightened.

His perception told him that her fear did not arise entirely from the fact that she had lost her memory.

There was some other reason.

But what it could be he had no idea.

chapter six

SITTING beside Anona in Lin Kuan Teng's carriage, Lord Selwyn calculated this would be the fifth time he had been to Durham House.

It was, however, the first time he had been able to take Anona there alone.

Twice she had come with Mrs. Teng and her daughters.

He had watched her and enjoyed hearing her laughing with the other girls.

But he had known then that he wanted to have her to himself.

There was so much to see, so much to explore at Durham House.

He knew it would take him weeks, if not months, to know it properly.

He had spent a number of hours there with the Solicitors, and also a few on his own.

Although he tried not to admit it, he knew that he wanted to show Anona his treasures when there was no one else there.

It was not just her beauty which intrigued him, or the fact that she had lost her memory.

There was something different which he could not explain.

It was almost as if she vibrated towards him.

He was aware of her personality in the same way that he had been aware of the Viceroy's.

Sometimes when they were talking and the conversation at table was extremely intelligent, he would look at Anona.

Their eyes would meet.

It would be as if they were speaking to each other without words.

Then he scoffed at being imaginative and told himself he was falling out of one trap into another.

But it was impossible not to think of Anona when he went to bed at night.

He would feel as if she were there in the moonlight seeping through his open windows.

He would talk to her about himself and his plans for the future.

"I am going crazy!" he said more than once. "I must be insane to think of another young woman after Maisie!"

He knew now that what he felt for Anona was very different from what he had felt for Maisie.

He could not explain it.

Yet while Maisie had seemed to him young, pure, and in some ways a child, Anona was very much a woman.

He was aware that Lin Kuan Teng was very impressed by her intelligence.

He was astonished at the amount she knew about the world, even though she could not remember travelling.

Lord Selwyn realised she was completely unselfconscious about her beauty.

The two Chinese girls laughed and talked with her as if she were their sister.

To-day Mrs. Teng and her two daughters had to attend a Concert.

It was taking place that afternoon at the School where they had been educated.

They had not invited Anona to go with them.

Lord Selwyn guessed it was because they did not want her to be embarrassed.

How could she explain that she had lost her memory and did not even know her name?

It was then he said:

"If you have nothing else to do, I would like you to accompany me to Durham House."

He saw her eyes light up, and she answered quickly:

"I would love that, for there are still a great many treasures I have not yet had time to see. I feel sure that must also apply to you."

Lord Selwyn admitted this was true.

There were not only the things he had seen first in the main rooms of the house.

There were a great number of other rooms which also contained Chinese porcelain.

One room was entirely devoted to porcelain of the Ch'ing Dynasty.

In another there were masks that had been used at Chinese festivals for hundreds of years.

Some were very ugly and some very attractive.

When he had gone to bed that night, Lord Selwyn

made a mental note of everything that he wanted to show to Anona.

He had a feeling that his treasures would mean more to her than they would to anybody else.

Then he told himself that once again he was being ridiculous.

She appreciated beautiful things as any other woman did.

Why then should he suppose that his possessions would have a special meaning for her that was different?

When morning came, he knew she was looking forward eagerly to going with him to Durham House.

At the same time, because he thought he should protect her reputation, he told Higgins he was to come too.

He saw his valet's expression as he spoke.

He knew that Higgins had been hoping to see the house.

Every day as he dressed his Master he had asked a number of leading questions.

Lord Selwyn had deliberately not allowed him to go there becuase he felt he was too curious.

Although he was aware of Higgins's delight, he said nothing.

They drove off after breakfast.

Anona was wearing a very attractive gown which Mrs. Teng had purchased for her in the town.

She was aware that there were Chinese tailors who could make things very quickly.

She had not expected, however, to have anything so pretty.

The gowns fitted her perfectly.

At first she had just one gown to wear, but after that they arrived almost hour by hour.

Anona thought it was as if they had been produced by magic.

There were gowns to wear in daytime made of a thin material with small bustles.

Then came three evening-gowns with large bustles in exquisite silks that could only have come from China.

"How can you give me anything so lovely?" she asked Mrs. Teng.

"Mr. Teng always say beautiful picture need beautiful frame," Mrs. Teng replied.

"You are both so kind," Anona said. "I feel very embarrassed at accepting so much from you."

She paused and then continued:

"Please persuade Mr. Teng to sell one of my bracelets to pay for all these things."

Mrs. Teng held up her hands in horror.

"You insult my husband! He think grave breach hospitality to accept payment from Honourable Guest."

Anona knew that this attitude was very true where the Chinese were concerned.

She could only therefore say over and over again:

"Thank you! Thank you!"

Secretly she was also pleased that she would not look peculiar in Lord Selwyn's eyes.

After all, they were both English.

She did not want him to think she was dressing in a strange fashion just to draw attention to herself.

Now they were travelling in one of Lin Kuan Teng's comfortable open carriages.

It had a fine lawn cover over their heads to protect them from the burning heat of the sun.

Higgins sat on the box beside the coachman, and as he was there they took no footman with them.

They drove down the main street of the town.

There were food-hawkers, fruit-vendors, pedlars, and side-walk book-sellers.

There were people drinking *kopi-o,* strong black coffee, under shady angsana trees.

The houses had great wooden shutters.

"It is very exciting to be going to your house with you," Anona said.

She smiled at him and continued:

"There are so many questions I want to ask you about your new possessions. But the Chinese girls always wanted to be in the garden."

"I also want to look at the garden," Lord Selwyn said, "but without so many other people in it."

"You are becoming like Mr. Lin Kuan Teng," Anona said as she smiled. "He always says he cannot think or feel when people are talking like parakeets!"

"That is what he said to me when I went to the house for the first time," Lord Selwyn replied. "He never spoke a word all the time we were driving there!"

"He is right," Anona agreed, "but I do not mind being compared to the Parakeets. They are so lovely!"

By now they had left the town and were out in the countryside.

She pointed to a tree they were just passing.

Lord Selwyn could see there were a number of Parakeets in the branches.

"Look!" Anona exclaimed. "There is the Blossom-

Headed Parakeet with its red-violet head and shoulders, and blue and yellow tail!''

Lord Selwyn caught a glimpse of it as they drove past, and Anona went on:

"I must see if I can find you one of the Hanging Parakeets. They are very small and mainly green. They sleep suspended like bats and look like a cluster of leaves.''

Listening, Lord Selwyn thought she might be English, but she undoubtedly knew Malaysia well.

He turned to her suddenly and asked:

"What is your name?''

Anona was looking up at the trees they were passing for more birds.

Without thinking, she answered automatically:

"An—''

She stopped.

"Go on,'' Lord Selwyn said very gently.

"Anona!''

She said her name in a low voice, then added quickly:

"I have remembered . . . my name! I have . . . remembered it . . . because you . . . asked me.''

"It is a beautiful name, and it suits you,'' Lord Selwyn said. "What else do you remember?''

"Nothing else . . . I remember . . . nothing . . . else!'' Anona said.

She spoke too quickly.

Lord Selwyn knew instinctively that she was not telling the truth.

He was, however, too tactful to press her.

Instead, he said:

"Now, Anona, we can talk more comfortably, and I

feel closer to you because I know your name. It is very awkward to keep saying "Hi, you!" when I want to attract your attention."

Anona laughed.

"You have never said that!"

"But I have had to think it," he replied, "and I would much rather say 'Anona.'"

He made her name sound very attractive, Anona thought.

Perhaps it was because he spoke in a deep voice that it gave her a strange feeling within her breast.

Durham House was looking both impressive and attractive.

The morning sun was turning the white stone with which it was built to gold.

Lord Selwyn knew without being told that Higgins was impressed.

When he had helped Anona out of the carriage at the front-door, Higgins drove with it to the stables.

"Now we can explore without being interruped," Anona said in an excited voice as they went into the hall.

They moved into the large Sitting-Room.

Anona ran to the cabinets to look at the jade and other treasures.

Lord Selwyn went to the window.

The flowers in the garden were exquisite, and, as always, there was a cloud of butterflies hanging above them.

Without turning round, he said:

"I think what we should do first, Anona, is to go and look at the waterfall, and I want you to see the orchids, too, because after luncheon it will be too hot."

"Yes, that is sensible," Anona agreed.

They walked out through the French windows onto the grass and moved through the beds of orchids.

The shrubs were in blossom and so were a number of the trees.

The largest Rafflesia—known flowers in Malaysia with their brilliant colours—were parasitic upon the woody vines of certain linas.

They were walking side by side, and Anona said:

"Could anything be more beautiful!"

Before Lord Selwyn could answer she stopped suddenly.

Putting out her hand, she drew him to a standstill.

"Look!" she said in a whisper. "Look!"

He followed the direction of her eyes.

Poised above the rocks of the small waterfall that was just ahead of them, there was a bird.

It was half-hidden by some of the foliage, but Lord Selwyn knew at once he was seeing a Bird of Paradise.

They stood in silence, watching it.

Then slowly, as if it were not frightened, it flew into the thicker branches of the trees.

"A Bird of Paradise in Paradise itself!" Anona murmured. "Because it has come here to you, I know you are especially blessed!"

"And which god should I thank for the blessing?" Lord Selwyn asked.

He thought as he spoke that Anona was as lovely as the Bird of Paradise.

He was quite prepared to believe that she was a goddess, and he would kneel at her feet.

"We shall have to ask Mr. Teng," Anona replied.

"The Malayans always believe that the Bird of Paradise brings them special blessings from the gods."

She smiled as she added:

"They put special food for them outside their houses. Unfortunately it is usually eaten by the greedy squirrels."

Lord Selwyn laughed.

"I am afraid that it is true of life! Those who are boisterous and greedy push aside those who are fastidiously selective."

"Is that what . . . you are?" Anona asked ingenuously.

"Of course!" he replied. "How could I be anything else?"

He was looking at her as he spoke.

As their eyes met they neither of them moved, and it was difficult to look away.

Then, as if she read his thoughts, the colour came into Anona's cheeks and she said quickly:

"Let us . . . look at the waterfall and see if there are any more surprises for you."

"What are you expecting to see?" he asked. "A special fish?"

"Perhaps it is greedy to ask too much," Anona replied, "but I am sure the waters here will have King-fishers. And, of course, the tiny Sun-birds, which are one of my favourites."

"Then we must try to find them," Lord Selwyn replied.

They spent a long time at the waterfall, then walked again among the orchids.

Lord Selwyn wanted to pick some for her, but Anona prevented him.

"Let them stay where they belong," she said. "I feel

128

that somehow they would resent going away from . . . Paradise.''

She hesitated before the last word, then smiled at him as she said it.

He thought as she stood surrounded by the orchids that she herself was definitely part of Paradise.

As he looked at her he wanted more than he had ever wanted anything before to kiss her.

Then he knew it might frighten her.

Also, as she had come with him alone and unchaperoned, it would be a very reprehensible thing to do.

"It is getting hot," he said in a different tone of voice, "and I think we should go back to the house."

She walked reluctantly but obediently onto the green grass.

They went back and entered the room they had left through the French window.

To Lord Selwyn's surprise, they had been so long in the garden that when he looked at the clock he saw it was nearly half-past-twelve.

"I will tell Higgins," he said, "that we will have luncheon at once. I expect he will have it all laid out for us."

They had brought their luncheon with them, and Lord Selwyn was sure it would be a delicious one.

He had told his host how much he appreciated the food, and Lin Kuan Teng had said:

"If you intend to stay in your house, My Lord, I will tell my Chef to find you somebody who can cook as well as he does."

"I am sure that would be impossible," Lord Selwyn replied.

"I appreciate the compliment," Lin Kuan Teng said as he smiled, "but my Chef, who has been with me many years, will teach him what he does not know."

"You are very gracious, but I am already deeply in your debt," Lord Selwyn replied.

He did not answer the question directly as to whether he would stay or go.

He was still undecided in his own mind.

"If we are going to have luncheon," Anona was saying, "I would like to go upstairs and wash my hands and remove my hat."

"Of course," Lord Selwyn agreed. "I think you know your way."

"The bedrooms are as beautiful as the other rooms in the house," she answered.

She smiled at him as she spoke.

As she turned away he watched her through the open door cross the hall and climb up the curved staircase.

He suppressed a desire to go with her simply because he did not like her to be out of his sight.

"How can I feel like this?" he asked, turning his face back towards the sun.

It seemed impossible when he remembered the anger he had felt when he had left England.

A century might have passed since he had walked back to his house in Park Lane seething with fury.

Now everything he had felt, thought, and suffered seemed to have disappeared into a mist.

All that was real was the sunshine, the orchids, a Bird of Paradise, and Anona.

"Luncheon's ready, M'Lord, when you are!"

It was Higgins speaking behind him and Lord Selwyn turned round.

"Well, Higgins, what do you think of my house?" he asked.

"It's a bit of all right, M'Lord, an' no mistake," Higgins replied. "We could make ourselves real comfortable 'ere, if it pleases Your Lordship!"

Lord Selwyn was astonished.

He thought that Higgins would be horrified at the idea of staying for long in a foreign land.

In all their journeys together, and there had been a great number of them, whenever he asked his opinion of a place, Higgins would say:

"It's all right, I suppose, M'Lord, but there's no place like 'ome, an' you can 'ave too much o' them 'Nignogs'!"

He would say the same whether they were in India, Turkey, Africa, or Europe.

Now Lord Selwyn was curious.

He was about to ask Higgins what he meant, when Anona returned.

She came into the room looking like the sun itself.

She swept every other thought from Lord Selwyn's mind.

"Luncheon is ready, Anona," he said.

"I am hungry, as I am sure you are," Anona replied, "and I am hoping Higgins has brought some of the delicious fruit juice, as I am also very thirsty."

There was fruit juice for Anona and a light gold wine for Lord Selwyn.

The food might have been ambrosia.

But Lord Selwyn had the idea that it was as difficult

for Anona to taste what she was eating as it was for him.

They would be talking on a subject which interested them both.

Suddenly their eyes would meet and neither of them could remember what they had been saying.

When they had finished they moved into the Drawing-Room.

It was furnished with a unique collection of red lacquer chairs and cabinets.

Anona realised they were over a thousand years old.

She told herself before they left the room that she wanted to spend a long time studying a large picture.

It covered most of one wall.

But as they rose from the table she had forgotten all about it.

She moved into the next room and Lord Selwyn followed her.

They were just about to sit down on one of the comfortable sofas when a Malayan came running through the open door.

"Come! Come!" he said to Lord Selwyn, pointing over his shoulder.

"What is wrong?" Lord Selwyn asked.

"Come!" the man repeated.

It was then Anona spoke to him in his own language, asking him what was the matter.

He gave a start of surprise because she could speak Malayan.

He went into a long, almost incoherent speech about an accident.

"What is he saying?" Lord Selwyn asked.

"There has been an accident," Anona explained, "but

I cannot understand whether it is to a person or an animal.''

''Tell him to take me there at once.''

Anona translated what Lord Selwyn had said.

The man gave what seemed to be a cry of relief and started to run back through the hall.

''Shall I come with you?'' Anona asked.

''No,'' he answered. ''Stay here. It is getting very hot outside.''

He smiled at her.

The Malayan was shouting:

''Come! Come!'' and he walked quickly into the hall.

As he went he picked up the broad-brimmed hat which he had left on a chair when he arrived.

Anona followed them slowly out through the front-door.

She watched them hurrying over the grass and down the garden towards the Plantation.

Then, as her eyes were on Lord Selwyn's broad back, taking one stride to the Malayan's two, she stiffened.

She had a frightening premonition of danger.

It was so strong, so vivid, she made a little murmur that was like a sound of pain.

She knew she must go after Lord Selwyn.

''I should have gone in the first place,'' she said aloud.

He could not speak the language.

Also, she was not certain what he would find, or to where he was being taken.

She only knew that every instinct in her body warned her of danger.

She glanced round for her bonnet, then remembered that she had left it upstairs in the bedroom.

'There must be a sunshade or an umbrella here!' she thought.

There was no sign of one in the hall.

She pulled open a door, thinking it would lead into a cloak-room.

To her surprise, there were stairs going down into darkness.

She guessed they led to the cellars of the house.

She was just about to shut the door and run upstairs, when she heard a voice.

It came from below and from a man speaking in Chinese.

"Is he going?" a man asked.

"Cheng leading him in right direction," came the reply. "They will cross stream by bridge and go into wood."

"Shall we leave now?" the first man enquired.

"No, wait till they out of sight," the other man answered. "When they reach wood you ford stream and go in at top. You kill him—it take long time find him."

"Wang Yen say 'Hide body.' ' "

"Yes," the other man replied. "You do that. Get ready. They soon reach bridge."

It was then that Anona realised what was happening, and the meaning of what she had overheard.

For a moment she felt paralysed with horror.

These men, whoever they were, intended to kill Lord Selwyn.

Then, almost as if her father were telling her what to do, she felt not panic-stricken but cool and calm.

Very quietly she shut the cellar-door, then ran to the kitchen.

134

As she expected, Higgins was there with the Care-takers.

They were an elderly couple, and the Chinese coachman was with them.

They were sitting at the table and looked up in surprise as Anona burst into the room.

"The Master is in danger, Higgins!" she cried. "Come quickly! We have to save him!"

Higgins jumped to his feet, picked up his coat which he had placed over the back of his chair, and put it on.

Then, as Anona turned to leave the Kitchen, she said to the Coachman in Chinese:

"Put the horses back between the shafts, and be ready to leave."

She turned, and followed by Higgins, ran back the way she had come.

She sped through the front-door, down the steps, and across the garden.

As she did so she saw, what seemed far away in the distance, that Lord Selwyn had reached the wooden bridge that spanned the stream.

Beyond it were the thick trees and the wood which ran down that side of the estate.

She knew it would be useless to call to him; her voice would not carry that far.

Instead, she ran as fast as possible over the ground, where its crop was just coming into leaf.

It was difficult not to fall, as she had to jump over one line of plants and then another.

She felt despairingly that it was slowing her progress.

She was getting breathless when she heard Higgins behind her say:

"It's all right, Miss. Don't fret. I've got me pistol with me."

She wanted to reply that a pistol would be no use if they were too late.

The man who had been told by Wang Yen to kill Lord Selwyn might have done so by the time they arrived.

She expected he would use one of the long, sharp knives which were traditional.

She ran on, jumping, keeping her balance, at the same time begging Lord Selwyn in her heart to wait for her.

She saw him walk along the bridge, then pause and stand with his back to her, looking downstream.

She was sure the Malayan was saying: "Come! Come!"

But she felt that Lord Selwyn's intuition, like hers, was warning him that something was wrong.

Then, as if the impatient cries of the Malayan aroused him, Lord Selwyn turned to walk into the wood.

It was then that Higgins shouted:

"M'Lord! M'Lord!"

His voice rang out.

But Anona felt despairingly that they were still too far away for Lord Selwyn to hear him.

As breathlessly she ran on, she was praying desperately, her lips moving.

"Stop . . . him! Please God . . . stop him! Oh . . . Papa, stop . . . him! He cannot . . . die! I must . . . save him!"

"M'Lord! M'Lord!"

Higgins was shouting at the top of his voice, although he was short of breath.

Lord Selwyn turned round.

Now he could see to his astonishment Anona's hair shining gold against the cultivated land.

He walked back across the bridge towards them as the Malayan was saying frantically:

"Come! Come! Come!"

Lord Selwyn paid no attention.

Then suddenly Anona was beside him so breathless that she put out her hands to hold on to him in case she should fall.

"What is it? What has happened?" he asked.

"You . . . are . . . in . . . danger!" Anona replied, her voice almost incoherent.

Lord Selwyn supported her with his hands.

"It is all right," he said quietly. "I am here and in no danger at the moment."

"If you are, M'Lord, I'll soon deal with it!" Higgins said, pulling his pistol from his pocket.

"Th-they . . . were going . . . to . . . kill you in the . . . wood!" Anona managed to say.

"How do you know that?" Lord Selwyn enquired.

"I . . . I over . . . heard two men . . . talking in the . . . cellar!"

Lord Selwyn looked over his shoulder at the wood behind him.

The Malayan was still there, but now he was looking apprehensive and unsure of himself.

It was obvious he was wondering what he should do.

Higgins, looking at him aggressively, walked onto the bridge, the pistol in his hand.

The Malayan saw it, gave a cry of fear, and ran into the wood.

He did not look back, but disappeared amongst the trees.

Anona was leaning against Lord Selwyn.

Her breath came fitfully from between her lips, and her breasts moved beneath her thin gown.

"It is all right," he said gently. "You have saved me from whatever was planned, and the sooner we go home the better."

"I . . . I was . . . so afraid I . . . would . . . not be . . . in time . . . and you would go . . . into the . . . wood!"

"But you have saved me!" Lord Selwyn said.

Anona raised her head and looked towards the wood.

"They may . . . shoot at . . . you," she said in a frightened tone.

"Then let us go back," Lord Selwyn replied.

He put his arm around her and helped her to walk back over the Plantation.

Higgins followed behind, looking repeatedly as he did so towards the wood, his pistol still in his hand.

By the time they reached the garden they could see the carriage waiting outside the front-door.

Lord Selwyn helped Anona into it.

Then he said to Higgins:

"I think the young Lady's bonnet is upstairs in one of the bedrooms."

"I'll get it, M'Lord."

Higgins disappeared into the house.

Lord Selwyn went to the back of the carriage to stand looking towards the wood.

He almost expected to see the men who had planned to assassinate him.

But there were only the birds, the butterflies, and the spruce plants.

When Higgins returned, he took Anona's bonnet from him and got into the carriage.

He did not give it to her, but threw it onto the seat opposite him.

Then, as Higgins jumped up beside the coachman, the horses moved off.

It was then Lord Selwyn put his arm round Anona and drew her close to him.

"Now tell me, my darling, exactly what you over-heard, and why you came to save me."

At the endearment she looked up at him in surprise.

He smiled as he said very softly:

"I love you, but I have been trying not to say so for a long time."

"Y-you . . . you . . . love me?"

He thought that her eyes looked as if they were lit with a thousand candles.

"I love you!" Lord Selwyn affirmed. "How can I help it? You are not only the most beautiful person I have ever seen, but I feel about you as I have never felt about any woman before."

He paused and then continued:

"You are a part of me—and I cannot live without you!"

"It . . . it . . . cannot be . . . true!" Anona said.

She spoke in a rapt voice that was like the song of a bird and added:

"How can you . . . love me . . . when you . . . do not even . . . know who . . . I am?"

Lord Selwyn smiled.

"What does it matter?" he asked. "The only thing that matters is that I have found you, when I was certain you did not exist."

Anona drew in her breath before she said:

"I knew . . . when I first . . . saw you that . . . you were . . . different and more wonderful than any other man I had . . . ever met."

"That is what I want you to believe," Lord Selwyn said, "and when we are alone I will tell you what I feel about you, and how different you are."

She looked at him, and he thought it was impossible for anyone to look so radiant and in a way not human.

Almost despite himself, because he knew he ought to wait before he said it, Lord Selwyn asked:

"When will you marry me, my darling? I want you with me—and alone!"

For a moment Anona just looked at him.

Then, like a shadow moving over the moon, the radiance faded from her face.

"No!" she said. "No, no! You . . . must not . . . say that!"

chapter seven

WHEN they arrived back in George Town Lord Selwyn was feeling bewildered.

He knew—and he could not be mistaken—that Anona loved him.

But it was impossible to understand why she refused to marry him.

It was, however, difficult to argue while they were in the carriage, and he merely said quietly:

"We will talk about this, my precious, when we are alone. In the meantime, we must deal with those men who wished to kill me."

He felt the shiver that ran through her, and knew she could feel like that only about somebody she loved.

The Chinese servants told them when they arrived that the "Master" was on the verandah.

Lord Selwyn and Anona hurried towards him and were relieved to find Lin Kuan Teng was alone.

He looked up when they appeared and said:

"Welcome, my Most Honoured Guests, but you are back earlier than I expected!"

"We have something very important to tell you," Lord Selwyn said.

Lin Kuan Teng indicated two chairs.

He sat down again on his high-back chair which looked like a throne.

Briefly, in as few words as possible, Lord Selwyn told him what had occurred.

Lin Kuan Teng listened in silence, then he said to Anona:

"Will you repeat the exact words you heard in Chinese?"

Anona clasped her hands together like a child before she began to speak slowly in Chinese:

She repeated word for word what she had heard the first man say, and the questions the other Chinese had asked him.

Then she said:

"Wang Yen say, 'Hide body.' "   ·

Lin Kuan Teng gave an exclamation.

"Are you sure that was the name?" he interrupted.

"Quite sure," Anona replied. "He said Wang Yen. I could not be mistaken."

"Then I can only say that you have been of tremendous service not only in saving the Honourable Lord Selwyn's life, but in helping everyone in Penang."

Anona looked at him in surprise, and he said:

"We have been searching for a long time for a Secret Society under the orders of a man we suspected to be Wang Yen, but we had no proof."

He paused before he added:

"They have committed murder after murder and have corrupted a large number of our young people with opium."

He looked at Lord Selwyn as he went on:

"It never struck any of us for one moment that he might be using your house. But now I see how useful it has been to him, and the reason they want to kill you is so that they can keep it unoccupied for themselves."

"You think they are using it as a meeting-place?" Lord Selwyn asked.

"From what I have heard, I am certain of it," Lin Kuan Teng replied, "and I know how delighted and grateful the authorities in George Town will be when I tell them what has been discovered."

He rose to his feet, saying:

"I will go at once and get soldiers sent to apprehend those who are still in Durham House and to arrest Wang Yen."

As he was still speaking, he had moved in his usual dignified way across the room.

At the same time, they were aware that he was in a hurry.

Only when he had gone out did Anona say almost as if she spoke to herself:

"Now they will not . . . try again to . . . kill you."

"If they do, you must save me," Lord Selwyn said as he smiled.

He thought she shook her head, and he said:

"Are you thinking of leaving me? I promise you it is impossible. You are mine, Anona, and I will never let you go."

There was a pause before she looked up at him, and her face was very pale.

"You . . . do not understand," she said in a strangled voice. "You must . . . forget me."

"Do you really think that is possible?" Lord Selwyn

demanded. "I love you, Anona, I love you, and whatever you may say, I intend to marry you!"

"But . . . you cannot . . . it is . . . impossible!"

She rose from her chair and walked across the room and out onto the verandah.

She stood between two of the pillars, looking out to sea.

As Lord Selwyn moved after her, he was aware that she was thinking that as she had come from the sea, she must leave by the sea.

"Wherever you go," he said softly, "I shall follow you."

A little tremor ran through her, but she did not turn her head.

"Y-you are . . . so important . . . there is so much for you to . . . do in the world . . . you must . . . forget me."

"I have nothing more important to do than to love you."

There was silence, and moving close behind her, he said:

"I love you, Anona! I love you until there is nothing else in the world but you."

His voice deepened as he went on:

"You are the sky, the sea, the earth, the birds, and besides all that to me you are Paradise!"

As he finished speaking, he put his arms around her.

Before she could prevent it, his lips were on hers.

She made one frantic little effort to escape.

Then, as if she could not help it, she surrendered herself to his kisses.

He found her lips, as he expected, soft, sweet, and innocent.

At first he was very gentle, as if he were touching a flower.

Then she aroused in him sensations he had never known he could feel, an ecstasy he had never experienced before.

His lips became more demanding and more passionate.

Anona could no longer think but only feel as her whole body melted into his.

The rapture that swept through her was like the sunshine.

As Lord Selwyn lifted her up to the sky she thought she really must have died and was in Paradise.

It was impossible for anyone to know such wonder and still be on earth.

Then, as his kiss turned to fire, she felt the sunshine within her turn to little flames.

They flickered through her breasts up to her lips.

Only when Lord Selwyn's feelings became too intense to bear did he raise his head.

In a voice that was curiously unlike his own, he asked:

"Now will you say you will marry me?"

Because she felt as if he drew her from Heaven back to earth, Anona could not speak.

She could only look at him, and her eyes were more eloquent than words.

"You love me," Lord Selwyn said, "oh, my darling, you love me! How can either of us fight against something so utterly and completely wonderful?"

"I love you . . . I do love you!" Anona said. "But . . . I cannot . . . marry you!"

The words were almost incoherent, and she hid her face against his shoulder.

He kissed her hair, thinking it was like silk, before he said:

"Tell me, my lovely one, why not? There must be a reason!"

"It is . . . s-something I can tell . . . no one!" Anona stammered.

"You must tell me," Lord Selwyn persisted. "Whatever your secret may be, you know I will keep it, and protect you."

There was silence, then in a voice he could hardly hear, Anona said:

"I . . . I can tell . . . no one and . . . because it will . . . hurt you . . . one of us must . . . go away."

Lord Selwyn put his fingers gently over Anona's chin and turned her face up to his.

There were tears in her eyes.

Yet when she looked up at him he saw the radiance behind them and knew how completely she loved him.

Never before had he seen a woman who radiated love as if it were a light shining from within her.

He knew, in fact, that it was a light that came from Anona's soul.

"My precious! My darling! My beautiful little goddess," he said, "how can you be so cruel to me?"

"I am . . . trying to be . . . kind by . . . thinking of you . . . and not of myself," Anona said in a broken little voice. "I would . . . kill myself . . . rather than . . . hurt you."

Lord Selwyn kissed her again.

As he did so, he told himself that whatever her secret might be, he would never leave her, never lose her.

He realised when she spoke of her secret that her memory was returning.

Or, what was more likely, she had never lost it in the first place.

Whatever it was, he vowed that he would look after her and love her for the rest of their lives.

* * *

A little while later they moved to a sofa at the far end of the verandah.

As they sat down, Anona put her head on Lord Selwyn's shoulder.

Holding her close against him, he said tenderly:

"You are tired, my precious one! You have been through too much. Just for a moment, let us forget the problems. Let us be content to be together."

"It is a . . . wonder beyond . . . wonders to be . . . with you," Anona murmured, "but . . . we have to be . . . sensible."

"It is sensible to be content with what we have," Lord Selwyn said. "All I ask of the gods is that I can hold you like this in my arms and know that you love me."

"I love you . . . I love you!"

She spoke softly; at the same time, it was a cry of despair.

Then, when Lord Selwyn was about to answer her, a servant appeared and he took his arms from her.

He was one of the Senior servants, and he bowed low as he said:

"Most Honourable Lord, visitor call to see you."

"A visitor?" Lord Selwyn questioned.

He thought perhaps it was someone sent by Lin Kuan

Teng to report what had happened at Durham House.

Then, as if he had asked the question, the servant explained:

"Visitor come ship."

Lord Selwyn looked puzzled, but there was nothing he could say but "Bring the visitor in."

As he spoke, he rose to his feet.

Leaving the sofa, he walked into the centre of the verandah so that Anona would not be involved.

It was only a few seconds before the servant returned, and with him was a man who was obviously English.

Lord Selwyn took one look at him, then exclaimed:

"Good gracious! Adrian Meredith! I was not expecting to see you!"

The Englishman, a man a little older than Lord Selwyn, laughed.

"I thought I would surprise you, My Lord! Actually, I left England soon after you did, and have been only five or six days behind you."

Lord Selwyn looked surprised, but replied:

"Sit down and tell me why you are here, and I am sure you would like some refreshment."

The servants had anticipated that would be required.

One of them appeared with a tray on which there was a decanter of wine and two glasses.

There was also a plate containing small delicacies like quails' eggs which were usually served with the drinks.

Lord Selwyn and Adrian Meredith picked up their glasses and the latter said:

"To your future, My Lord, which is why I am here!"

"My future?" Lord Selwyn enquired.

"Three days before I left London," Adrian Meredith

replied, "the Secretary of State for Foreign Affairs, Lord Clarendon, was informed that owing to ill health, the Governor of Singapore wished to retire."

He paused to glance at Lord Selwyn before he went on:

"His Lordship therefore instructed me to follow you. I am authorised to offer you the post, for which he thought you would be admirably suited."

Lord Selwyn seemed to be turned to stone, and Adrian Meredith continued:

"Lord Clarendon's recommendation was confirmed by the Prime Minister, and Mr. Disraeli asked me to tell you that he personally would be gratified if you would accept the Governorship."

Lord Selwyn was still silent.

Then, with an effort to find his voice, he said:

"You will understand that this has come as a tremendous surprise. In fact, it has never struck me for one moment that my services might be required in the East."

Adrian Meredith smiled and said:

"I am sure Your Lordship knows better than I do that Singapore is becoming not only the most important Trading Post in the whole of Asia, but its development is essential to the Empire."

He paused, then went on with an almost boyish enthusiasm:

"I can imagine no one who could fill the post better than you, My Lord! Considering the brilliance with which you have executed so many difficult missions in the past."

He paused, smiling, before he continued:

"I know you are exactly the right man at this particular moment for Singapore."

"Thank you!" Lord Selwyn said. "And I am very grateful to you for having come so far."

He saw an apprehensive look on Adrian Meredith's face.

He thought he was going to refuse outright what had been suggested.

"What I would like to do," Lord Selwyn said, "is to sleep on the proposition, and consider it carefully."

He rose to his feet.

"I know you must be tired after such a long journey. May I suggest that you rest and return to-morrow morning, when I know my host will be delighted to welcome you."

He paused thoughtfully, and then said:

"I hope then to have my answer ready for you to take back with you to England."

Adrian Meredith finished his wine and put down the glass.

"I quite understand, My Lord," he said, "that this has been a shock, but I can only beg you to consider the proposal carefully and, if humanly possible, favourably. We really need you."

Lord Selwyn was touched by the way he spoke, but he merely smiled somewhat enigmatically.

He walked from the verandah into the house, and there was nothing Adrian Meredith could do but follow him.

The carriage in which he had come was waiting at the front-door.

"You have somewhere to stay?" Lord Selwyn enquired.

"Yes, thank you," Adrian Meredith replied. "It has been arranged with the Resident."

Lord Selwyn held out his hand.

"Then goodbye until to-morrow, Meredith, and thank you again for following me."

"Oh, I forgot to tell you," Adrian Meredith exclaimed. "I stopped in Calcutta on my way here and, of course, in confidence, I told the Viceroy, who I know is a friend of yours, the reason for my visit."

Lord Selwyn's eyes twinkled.

He remembered his conversation with the Earl of Mayo and knew exactly what he would have said.

"The Viceroy told me to tell you," Adrian Meredith continued, "that he has found in life that it is useless to oppose Fate. He said you would understand."

"I do!" Lord Selwyn laughed.

Meredith moved towards the carriage.

Then, as he was about to step inside, he picked up a newspaper that was lying on the seat.

"I bought this at my last port of call," he said, "and I thought it would interest you, as it seems there is another English hero in this part of the world."

He handed the newspaper to Lord Selwyn and got into the carriage.

As the horses moved off, he raised his hand in what was almost a salute.

Holding the newspaper, Lord Selwyn turned and walked back the way he had come.

Anona was still where he had left her, sitting on the sofa at the end of the verandah.

He knew, because she had been so quiet and inconspicuous, that Adrian Meredith had not been aware she was there.

Lord Selwyn walked towards her.

Flinging the newspaper down on the chair, he put his arms around her.

He did not speak, and after a moment she said:

"I am so . . . glad that you have been offered something . . . so . . . important. The last Governor has not been . . . a success. Because he was never very well . . . he only . . . came to Singapore . . . occasionally."

"And you think it is the sort of post I should accept?" Lord Selwyn asked.

"Of course you must!" she replied. "You will be . . . wonderful and everybody will . . . admire and love . . . you. Papa always said that what . . . happened in Singapore directly . . . affected the whole trading system of the Empire."

Lord Selwyn noted that she had mentioned her father, but he asked quietly:

"Do you really want me to take this post?"

"I know you would be . . . magnificent in it—another Sir Stamford Raffles—and that is . . . exactly what is . . . needed."

"Then I will accept what I have been offered and promise to take up the Governorship as soon as I am married and have had my honeymoon."

He spoke very quietly, but there was a determination in his words that Anona did not miss.

"No . . . no!" she cried. "You know . . . I cannot . . . marry you . . . especially if . . . you are the . . . Governor of Singapore."

"Why not, my precious?"

There was silence, and Lord Selwyn said:

"Very well, as I have no intention of living in the East without a wife, I will explain to Adrian Meredith and the Foreign Secretary why I cannot accept the honour."

Anona gave a little cry:

"You must not do . . . that! You . . . cannot do . . . that! How can I make you . . . understand that I dare not . . . marry you?"

"You can do that quite easily," Lord Selwyn answered, "by telling me your secret."

There was silence again.

Then Anona moved from his arms to stand as she had before between two of the pillars, looking out into the garden.

Lord Selwyn did not touch her, but she could feel him come and stand just behind her.

She felt as they vibrated so closely to each other that it was impossible for them to be separated.

Then she knew that whatever else she did, whatever happened to her, she could not spoil his life.

She could not endanger his career through her father's crime.

She clasped her hands together as if to give herself strength.

Feeling as if she might faint with the horror of what she had to do, she said in a small voice he could hardly hear:

"I . . . I will . . . tell you the . . . truth."

Because he knew what she was feeling, Lord Selwyn came even closer to her.

"I hate to upset you, my precious," he said. "At the

same time, this concerns us both, and it is something from which neither of us can escape."

"I . . . know," Anona replied, "but . . . when you hear what I have to . . . tell you . . . you will understand why we . . . can never see each other . . . again."

"And you really think that is what will happen?" Lord Selwyn asked.

"I . . . know . . . it will," she said.

She turned round unexpectedly.

He thought he had never seen such suffering in a woman's face, such pain in her eyes.

"My darling," he said.

"Kiss me," Anona whispered. "Kiss me . . . for the . . . last time . . . and remember when you . . . leave me that I shall be . . . praying for you and . . . loving you . . . until I . . . d-die."

She moved a little nearer, and Lord Selwyn swept her into his arms.

Then his lips took her captive.

He kissed her not gently, but fiercely, demandingly, possessively.

He was, she knew, fighting her with kisses, and she surrendered herself completely.

She felt as if she gave him her body, her heart, and her soul, and there was nothing left.

He kissed her, then, as if the strain were too intense to be borne any longer, he set her free.

She held on to the stone wall in front of her as if she were afraid she might fall.

Then, as Lord Selwyn moved so that he did not actually touch her, she said in a strange, frightened little voice:

"M-my father is . . . Captain Guy Ranson . . . formerly

of the Royal Navy. Because he . . . needed money for . . . my mother and . . . myself he became . . . a . . . Pirate!''

She spoke hardly above a whisper.

But she felt as if the last word rang out like the cry of doom into the garden.

Lord Selwyn did not move or speak, and she went on:

''He . . . made a lot of . . . money holding cargo vessels to ransom and called himself a 'Highwayman in a ship' rather than on a horse. . . . He extracted payment from the Captains of the vessels in return for not harming them or stealing their cargo.''

It was difficult for Anona to continue, and she drew a deep breath before she went on.

She did not look at Lord Selwyn.

He had not moved since she started her story.

''My father and two of his friends who worked with him boarded a ship one night, and he . . . he encountered an Englishman who had been in the Navy with him . . . and was sure he had been . . . recognised.''

There was a sob in Anona's voice as she went on:

''To save me from . . . being classed as the . . . daughter of a . . . criminal who would . . . be hanged if he was . . . caught . . . he sent me to Lin Kuan Teng, who is a friend of his . . . although Mr. Teng does not . . . know who I am.''

She made a little gesture with her hands before she finished:

''Th-that is . . . why I am . . . h-here . . . you . . . know the rest!''

As she finished speaking she shut her eyes.

She was waiting for the sound of Lord Selwyn's footsteps walking away from her in disgust.

Then his arms went round her.

He was holding her close against him and he was kissing her eyes, her cheeks, and then her lips.

Only when she felt as if she had stepped from a Hell of despair back into Paradise did Lord Selwyn say:

"My darling! My sweet! My lovely one! Do you really think that what your father did or did not do is of any significance? I love you! I would love you if you yourself were a Pirate!"

Anona looked up at him in wonder.

"D-do you . . . really mean . . . that?"

"Of course I mean it!" he said. "I understand now why you have been so frightened, and why you had to pretend to lose your memory."

"But . . . how can you possibly . . . marry somebody who is . . . anonymous?"

"We will think of something," Lord Selwyn said confidently, "and of one thing I am quite certain—people, however inquisitive or suspicious, will not argue with the Governor!"

He spoke jokingly, but instead of laughing Anona burst into tears.

She hid her face against him, and he could feel her whole body trembling.

"It is all right, my precious, my darling," he said.

"I know how frightened you have been, and ashamed of telling me. But it does not matter—honestly and truly—it does not matter to me."

He kissed her cheek and then continued:

"If you had committed a hundred murders, I would still love you and want to marry you."

"I-is . . . that true?" Anona sobbed. "N-no man . . . can be so . . . wonderful!"

"You have to believe in me," Lord Selwyn said. "I adore you, and we are going to be married immediately!"

"You are . . . making a mistake . . . I cannot let you . . . do anything that would . . . hurt you."

"The only thing that would hurt me would be if you stopped loving me and left me alone."

He looked down at her.

"I am not joking when I tell you that if you do that, I shall go straight back to England, whatever you or anybody else may say!"

"But . . . Singapore . . . needs you!"

"And I need you!"

He kissed her again to stop any more protests.

Only when her tears had gone and her eyes were shining did he say:

"Now—tell me you will marry me!"

"What . . . can I do? What can I . . . say?"

"Just one word," he answered. " 'Yes!' "

"You are making . . . a mistake!" Anona stammered.

"I shall spend a lifetime showing you that you are wrong," he replied.

He kissed her again. Then he said:

"As I want to go on talking to you, my precious one, and as I think time is getting on, let us go into the garden and down to the bay, where I first saw you, and where we will not be interrupted."

"That would be lovely," Anona said, "but I first want to . . . bathe my eyes . . . because I . . . want to . . . look pretty for you."

Anona turned her face up to his.

157

"You are more beautiful every time I look at you," he said, "and every day I fall more and more in love!"

"That . . . is what I feel too," she whispered.

"Then hurry," he told her, "because I want to be alone with you, and at any moment our host and his family may be coming back."

Anona gave a little cry and moved away from him.

She had just reached the centre of the Sitting-Room which opened off the verandah when she heard Lord Selwyn call out:

"Anona—wait! Anona!"

She turned back.

"Come here! I have something to show you."

She went back to him, and as he put his arm around her she was aware that he was holding a newspaper in his hand.

It was the one Adrian Meredith had given him.

Lord Selwyn held it so that Anona could see the headlines.

She read:

> ENGLISH HERO SAVES
> VOYAGERS FROM PIRATES
> *Captain Guy Ranson's*
> *Brave Defeat of the Prahus*

Anona read the Headlines, then gave a little cry.

"Papa! It is about Papa!"

The fear was back in her eyes, but Lord Selwyn drew her down on the sofa.

Then he read aloud what was printed below the head-lines.

It appeared that one of Captain Ranson's friends had been taken ill.

Although they had been in the Malaccan Sea, he had turned for home.

He was on his way to take his friend to the Hospital in Singapore, and it was getting late.

It was then they saw by chance two ship-loads of *Prahus*, the most dangerous Pirates known.

They were boarding a pleasure cruiser which had anchored for the night in one of the quiet bays in the Straits.

Captain Ranson realised the *Prahus* would kill every-body aboard before stealing everything they owned.

With the other Englishmen aboard and four members of his crew, they fought the *Prahus* as they crept aboard.

They managed to kill quite a number of them and the rest retreated.

Then, as he came to the last paragraph, Lord Selwyn paused before he read:

Unfortunately, at the very moment of victory, a long knife, the favourite weapon of the Prahus, pierced Captain Ranson's chest. The ship he had saved took him as swiftly as possible towards Singapore but he died from loss of blood.

Everyone acknowledges that it was an extremely heroic act on the part of the ex-Naval Captain.

A petition has been forwarded to London, asking

Her Majesty the Queen to reward in some appro-
priate manner the courage both of Captain Ranson
and of his friend, Lieutenant Hutchinson. It was
their swift action which undoubtedly saved the lives
of more than thirty people who invited contributions
towards the memorial to the brave Captain. This
would be erected in Singapore.

As he finished reading, Lord Selwyn threw down the
newspaper and put his arms around Anona.

She was crying.

But now the tears running down her cheeks were, he
understood, in some way tears of gladness.

That her father had died in such an heroic manner was
how she wanted to remember him.

There was now no danger of his being hanged as a
criminal.

"You must not be unhappy, my darling," Lord Selwyn said gently. "I am sure it was the way your father
would have wished to die, and now he knows that I will
look after you."

"That would be . . . what Papa . . . would want," Anona answered.

"Of course he would, and I think, too, he would be
very proud to know that you will be helping to govern
Singapore in exactly the way it should be governed."

Anona made a little sound that was half a laugh and
half a sob.

Then, with her face against Lord Selwyn's neck, she
whispered:

"Can I . . . really be your . . . wife?"

"I had every intention of marrying you whatever your connections might be," Lord Selwyn replied, "but I am very proud, my darling, that my wife should be the daughter of a hero, a man who will go down in history admired and acclaimed by everybody who learns how he died."

"It . . . it cannot be true that this has . . . happened, and I need no . . . longer be afraid that Papa may be . . . hanged."

"It is something we will never speak of again," Lord Selwyn said firmly. "He has proved himself a true Englishman, and no man could ask for a finer epitaph."

He drew Anona even nearer to him and said:

"All we have to do now, my precious, is to tell everybody who you are, and then we will find Paradise alone together."

"It will be Paradise . . . if I am . . . married to . . . you!" Anona whispered.

"It is what we have already found here in Penang," Lord Selwyn said. "We will spend our honeymoon at Durham House and we will holiday here whenever we can escape from our duties."

His lips were very near to hers as he said:

"I think, too, my lovely darling, that our children will enjoy Penang, and although we will have to return to England when my appointment is over, we will come back to our Paradise which will be waiting for us."

Anona looked up at him.

He thought the light in her eyes was the Divine Light which would lead, inspire, and guide him for the rest of his life.

As he kissed her again, Lord Selwyn knew that he had found what all men seek.

It is the love which is pure, perfect, and undefiled, the love which comes from God, and is eternal.

ABOUT THE AUTHOR

Barbara Cartland, the world's most famous romantic novelist, who is also an historian, playwright, lecturer, political speaker and television personality, has now written over 512 books and sold over 500 million copies all over the world.

She has also had many historical works published and has written four autobiographies as well as the biographies of her mother and that of her brother, Ronald Cartland, who was the first Member of Parliament to be killed in the last war. This book has a preface by Sir Winston Churchill and has just been republished with an introduction by Sir Arthur Bryant.

Love at the Helm, a novel written with the help and inspiration of the late Earl Mountbatten of Burma, Great Uncle of His Royal Highness The Prince of Wales, is being sold for the Mountbatten Memorial Trust.

She has broken the world record for the last fourteen years by writing an average of twenty-three books a year. In the *Guinness Book of Records* she is listed as the world's top-selling author.

Miss Cartland in 1978 sang an Album of Love Songs with the Royal Philharmonic Orchestra.

In private life Barbara Cartland, who is a Dame of the Order of St. John of Jerusalem, Chairman of the St. John

Council in Hertfordshire and Deputy President of the St. John Ambulance Brigade, has fought for better conditions and salaries for Midwives and Nurses.

She championed the cause for the Elderly in 1956 invoking a Government Enquiry into the "Housing Conditions of Old People."

In 1962 she had the Law of England changed so that Local Authorities had to provide camps for their own Gypsies. This has meant that since then thousands and thousands of Gypsy children have been able to go to School, which they had never been able to do in the past, as their caravans were moved every twenty-four hours by the Police.

There are now fourteen camps in Hertfordshire and Barbara Cartland has her own Romany Gypsy Camp called Barbaraville by the Gypsies.

Her designs "Decorating with Love" are being sold all over the U.S.A. and the National Home Fashions League made her, in 1981, "Woman of Achievement."

She is unique in that she was one and two in the Dalton list of Best Sellers, and one week had four books in the top twenty.

Barbara Cartland's book *Getting Older, Growing Younger* has been published in Great Britain and the U.S.A. and her fifth cookery book, *The Romance of Food*, is now being used by the House of Commons.

In 1984 she received at Kennedy Airport America's Bishop Wright Air Industry Award for her contribution to the development of aviation. In 1931 she and two R.A.F. Officers thought of, and carried, the first aeroplane-towed glider airmail.

During the War she was Chief Lady Welfare Officer in Bedfordshire looking after 20,000 Service men and women. She thought of having a pool of Wedding Dresses at the War Office so a Service Bride could hire a gown for the day.

She bought 1,000 gowns without coupons for the A.T.S., the W.A.A.F.'s and the W.R.E.N.S. In 1945 Barbara Cartland received the Certificate of Merit from Eastern Command.

In 1964 Barbara Cartland founded the National Association for Health of which she is the President, as a front for all the Health Stores and for any product made as alternative medicine.

This is now a £650 million turnover a year, with one third going in export.

In January 1988 she received *La Médaille de Vermeil de la Ville de Paris*. This is the highest award to be given in France by the City of Paris. She had sold 25 million books in France.

In March 1988 Barbara Cartland was asked by the Indian Government to open their health resort outside Delhi. This is almost the largest health resort in the world.

Barbara Cartland was received with great enthusiasm by her fans, who fêted her at a reception in the city and she received the gift of an embossed plate from the Government.